IMMORTAL SPARTAN

H.M. McQueen

HM McQueen 2019

Immortal Spartan
H.M. McQueen

Cover Artist: Dar Albert
Sr. Editor: Scott Moreland
Line Editor: Dark Dreams Editing

Copyright © Hildie McQueen 2019

ISBN: 978-1-939356-81-9

DEDICATION

I dedicate this story to my dear author friend Gayla Leath.
Thank you for believing in me, and your constant support.

CHAPTER ONE

T HANKS TO THE streetlights, Roderick Bronan could see what went down clearly. Not everyday one got to witness a sex against the wall scene. His Gore-Tex biker boots crunched noisily on the gravel as he moved closer. Queue the loud throat clearing. Nope the couple was too busy going at it and didn't hear him approach.

The blue tinge of the males skin was a clear giveaway. A dark Fae, or more commonly called a demon. Shit, sometimes killing one could be awkward. Like right now for instance. Did he clear his throat again and allow the couple to disengage before striking down the male? Or maybe behead the fucker while he was in full throttle. Either way it would probably send the female into hysterics.

Shit.

The woman moaned, definitely enjoying the tryst. "What are you doing?" his partner's voice hissed in his earpiece.

Roderick moved away from the couple. Other than some pretty gritty sex, the male was not feeding on the woman. She wasn't in danger at the moment. "I'm trying to decide when to kill a demon. Before or after he gets off."

Cynden Fraser's Scottish accented voice came across loud

and clear. "I hate when that happens. Why don't people get a room? Heading your way now, nothing much going down over here."

Instead of watching the action, Roderick stalked around the corner and leaned on the building. He pulled his headphones on and instants later Dr. Dre's voice boomed in his ears. Who would have thought a centuries old Spartan would be listening to rap at night while stalking around the moonlit streets of Atlanta hunting monsters that came out to kill, fuck or just cause trouble when needing to feed.

Then there was the messed up realization humans, his original race, were more like cattle upon which others preyed. And wasn't that a bitch?

THAT HE COULD separate himself from all of them, human or otherwise was sometimes good. Sure he was immortal and from a people that no longer existed, but first and foremost he'd been human. Funny what centuries of living did to a person.

Out of the corner of his eye his partner came into view. Spitting out sunflower seed shells as he scanned the side streets. No one would be stupid enough to bother the huge Scot. Blond with icy blue eyes, he'd never be mistaken for anything other than a badass biker.

Roderick cut off his music and waited for Cyn to approach. As his partner passed the side street, the Scot peered in and his eyebrows hitched. His lips twitched as he approached Roderick. "Damn they're having a good time. Too bad for them, it's about to be interrupted." He motioned with his head across the street where a patrol car pulled up and two officers got out. With purposeful strides, the cops crossed the street toward the couple.

Other than a wary glance in their direction, the boys in blue continued on toward the still oblivious couple.

Cyn laughed. "Someone must have reported them. Good citizens trying to get a good night's sleep and what do they hear? Sex noises outside their window."

Roderick nodded. "Someone's head banging against the glass is sure to interrupt a good slumber. Look, let's go check that out." He watched a new scene unfold across the street. Dark figured intruders climbed through a second story window. "Break in or something else?"

"Why would anyone break into an abandoned warehouse? Hmmm, maybe it's a party. I'm hurt we didn't get invited." Cyn continued rambling as they went around the back of the industrial looking building. "Could be one of those clubs that fly under the radar. Gotta love the Atlanta nightlife."

"Shut up Cyn," Roderick whispered as they approached from the dark alleyway.

"Shutting."

"Too many of them," Roderick said. They looked through a half broken dirty window.

A couple dozen demons congregated inside. They'd collected old couches and tables. Not seeming comfortable, they moved around the large room not speaking to each other. Instead they appeared to be waiting for some sort of announcement.

"Looks like some sort of meeting," Cyn whispered. "I'll buzz Thor and the Moor." He jogged away to make the call.

THANKS TO THEIR keen night vision, darkness was their friend. Not only did the world become clearer, but also every action seemed magnified, as if slower. As the Protectors burst through the doorway into the large dank warehouse, chaos broke out.

Swords were drawn, the sounds of metal slashing out of scabbards resounding as if choreographed. The flashes of the meager light reflected off the long blades adding to the ambience of danger and beauty. It was a dark beauty, which could only be appreciated by killers and fighters.

Thor's battle roar echoed louder than the curses and groans of pain. Roderick's long silver hair sailed around him as his sword sliced through a demon that flew at him. Just as a demon went to cut Cyn down, the stealthy Moor, whose presence had yet to register to most of the fighters, took it down.

Outside a car drove by, its loud thumping of the bass speakers filtering into the room; the bumps of each drumbeat sending vibrations into the empty warehouse. Cyn growled as he pulled his broadsword from the chest of a demon and lifted it up across his face to deflect a strike.

From across the room Roderick met Thor's luminescent gaze for a second, both turned to the side and simultaneously cut down demons, then looked back at each other and grinned like idiots.

Roderick crossed the space and scanned to ensure they'd not missed anything. Thor looked past him to where Cyn fought three. "Should we help him?"

"Nah, he needs the training," Roderick replied, but kept an eye on his partner to ensure he wasn't in trouble. "Looks like he's down to two now."

Thor nodded, attention on a nasty gash on his left shoulder. "One of the bloody bastards got lucky."

"Getting slow Viking?"

"Fuck you." Thor frowned. "Where's the Moor? He better not have left me."

"Rode bitch?"

"Hell no. We were out in his Jeep. Night off, were about to have dinner."

It was hard to picture a Viking and a silent Moor out to dinner. Maybe a biker bar, or a diner, but he couldn't picture them at Olive Garden.

Cyn neared, his chest expanding and contracting with each breath. "You fuckers could have given me a hand."

Thor shrugged and Roderick attempted not to laugh. "Yeah? We figured you had matters under control. Thor got sliced, so I was checking on him."

"Whatever; since when did you become Florence Nightingale?" Cyn stalked away. "We need to get rid of any bodies left."

With daggers fisted they struck the demons in the chest. Immediately each one evaporated; blue smoke the only evidence they'd existed. Well, that and the smell, a combination of rotted eggs and tar.

They hurried through a now doorless entryway. Roderick took a deep breath when they walked outside. "That's some awful shit."

A black Jeep pulled up and Cyn neared it. The Moor, with long dreads and a scowl, hitched his chin in greeting. It was the closest to a bright smile they'd ever get from him.

"Hey Rowe. Where you going to eat?" Cyn was oblivious to the Moor's scowl. "I'm hungry."

Thor answered for his partner. "We were heading to an all night diner. He likes one of the waitresses."

The comment earned Thor a scowl, but other than that, silence as usual.

"I don't think we need to be around anyone right now. We stink." Roderick told them.

Cyn nodded. "True. I'm thinking we're more along the lines of ordering pizza right now."

Roderick looked back to the building. "They're organizing. Never seen so many coming together. We should let Julian know."

"Maybe it was a one time thing," Cyn said but by his lowered brows, he'd thought the same thing.

Thor let out a groan. "That's all we need. If hundreds of them get organized, we're screwed."

The truth was stark at times.

CHAPTER TWO

A TLANTA HOLIDAY TRAFFIC was a killer. Rachel Andrews held her breath and floored the accelerator to get from in between two tractor-trailers. Her cell phone chirped and she hit the answer key on her steering wheel while watching a car zigzag between two other cars in an attempt to get to the nearest exit.

"Hello."

"Hey girl, did you make it out of town yet?" Her best friend Deborah's voice came over the car speakers. In the background she could hear the hum of voices and jazz. Her friend worked part time at a local club as a bartender on weekends. It made Rachel smile to know the PhD liked to spend her days off pouring drinks. "Hellooo?" Deborah repeated.

"Hell no I'm not out of town. It's bumper-to-bumper traffic. I'm barely past Alpharetta. I figure another few miles and the traffic should cut down drastically. Not many people go to the wine country for the holidays. This time of year its cold and rainy."

"I still can't believe you're going alone. Why would you want to spend Thanksgiving by yourself in a cabin? I'm so sorry I had to cancel, but with my parents visiting from Chicago…"

"Stop apologizing. I'm looking forward to a week in the mountains. I plan to catch up on sleep and reading."

"Sounds delightful." There was a wistfulness in Deborah's voice. They talked for a few minutes and by the time her friend hung up the traffic had lightened up considerably.

The setting sun made it hard to see clearly. Rachel dug in her purse with one hand then cursed when the bag fell off the seat and onto the floorboard with all of the contents spilling. Thankfully there was a wide shoulder so she pulled over.

Just as she bent to pick up her belongings someone knocked on the window. Rachel jerked upward to see an attractive man standing back, his hands deep in his jeans pockets. He gave her a crooked smile and shrugged as if apologizing for startling her.

There hadn't been anyone walking on the roadside, she was sure of it. She looked in her rearview mirror but didn't see a car parked behind her. Her finger lingered over the window controller, but then she figured cracking it a bit to talk to him wouldn't hurt.

"Sorry to scare you. I broke down and am heading to the next exit for gas. I could use a ride. My girlfriend always leaves the car almost empty."

Rachel looked to where the next exit sign showed it was a mile further down the road. Not too bad of a walk, but it was drizzling and forty degrees. His hair was wet and his nose red from the cold.

"Look don't worry about it. I'll walk. I totally understand you not feeling comfortable with it." He turned and began walking, his back hunched.

Rachel put the car in drive and pulled up alongside the poor guy. "Come on. I'll take you, it's just up the road."

Once he settled into the seat, he turned to her and held out his hand. "I'm Ryan."

Something about his gaze made her blink and focus on him. For an instant she'd thought to have seen a red rim around his irises. Probably the setting sun. Rachel looked to her side mirror to pull back onto the road when all of a sudden Ryan bent forward and groaned.

"Are you all right?" Rachel touched his shoulder. "Please don't tell me you're going to throw up in my car."

"No. I'm not going to do that, but you might."

Moments later as she faced certain death, two thoughts struck Rachel Andrews. Her mother's warning to never pick up hitchhikers and…well I'll be damned, monsters really do exist.

With amazing speed, razor sharp talons slashed through her seatbelt and the hellish creature somehow dragged her between the seats toward the back seat. Rachel struggled to grip on to something, anything.

He was too strong.

Her scream echoed in the car. She continued to yell even though she knew with the windows up and fogging they weren't visible and no one would hear her. One thing was for certain, she didn't plan to die this day. Rachel used every strike she'd learned in self-defense class, but the monster didn't seem to feel any pain or discomfort. His red eyes remained focused on her throat. In desperation, she continued to scratch and kick at her assailant without avail.

As he pushed her down onto the seat, Rachel continued to fight until so exhausted she was barely able to lift her leaden arms. Forcing her body to relax for a moment, she concentrated on catching her breath and not allowing fear to cloud her mind. Maybe she could still survive.

Red-rimmed eyes scanned over her face making every inch of her skin crawl. At the same time his claws cut into her left shoulder, pinning her to the back seat.

"Pl-please take my car and my purse…but don't kill me." Her words were a hoarse rasp working past the constriction on her throat by his other hand.

His lips peeled back to reveal elongated fangs. With a stifled gulp, she recoiled further into the leather seat.

"Oh but those last drops of blood when life ebbs out of your body are the sweetest. You don't expect me to deny myself of that would you?" Saliva dripped from his incisors. His horrifying gaze focused on her throat next and with a primal growl, he shoved her face to the side.

When the demon's teeth broke her skin, a desperate scream tore deep from within her chest. Survival instincts kicked in and once again she began to kick and punch at the demon. Her feeble attempts to shove him off didn't seem to register and his hold remained tight. It fed with greed, each pull of her blood bringing her closer to death.

Suddenly the creature evaporated. A thick blue mist took

its place and the smell of something like rotted eggs engulfed the interior of the car.

Through the haze of tears and smoke, a huge figure loomed over her.

Whether real or a hallucination brought on by her brain as an escape mechanism when she neared death, Rachel wasn't sure. Striking silver eyes met hers, matching long hair framed the angelic man's face.

"Can you hear me?" His deep voice resonated and his fingers pressed against her throat. Was he feeling for a pulse? "It's going to be all right. I'm here to take you to safety."

Rachel couldn't reply, but her mind was awhirl. For the first time in four years, she'd taken vacation from the library to make it only a few miles away from home, to the outskirts of Atlanta.

Later perhaps it would strike her as interesting what her last thoughts were. She should have stopped by to see her mother, the only person she hated leaving. Why had she not made plans to spend the holiday with her instead? Or stopped by to see her one last time? Her mom would be desolate and alone without her.

Rachel's vision began to fade, if only the searing pain at her throat would fade too. The burning at the spot where the demon fed brought a shudder. *God make it stop.*

The male before her had to be Death; he'd come for her. She was dying—the sooner the better. Then the agony would stop.

The large angel of death began to blur. It was her time and she prepared herself. Would he take her away immediately?

Who would notify her mother? Oh God, would it hurt? She opened her mouth to ask him questions, but instead a fog fell.

THE TUNNEL WAS long and dark. Mist swirled around like the inside of a tornado, and in the far distance was a shining beacon of light. Rachel struggled to float toward it, but the opening got further away when she moved forward. Battling with all her might, she was finally able to reach the entrance and emerge.

Prying heavy eyelids open, the surroundings came into focus. She lay in the middle of an enormous four-poster bed in an unfamiliar bedroom. Rachel scanned the area from under her lashes. The brightness from outside the cracked doorway provided just enough light for her to see. She was not alone.

The angel from inside her car moved about the space. Barely able to contain the instinctual gasp, she watched him. The massive death angel was in the room with her.

A towel wrapped low around his hips, he swore and dug through a drawer. "Where the hell are my damn shorts?"

He had to be well over six foot tall, closer to seven feet if she were to guess. His broad muscular back bunched and his biceps bulged with each motion. He closed the drawer slowly and opened another. Letting out a breath, he pulled out a pair of grey gym shorts. When his towel slipped he didn't bother to tighten it, instead he let it fall to the floor. Her eyes widened at the sight of his bare bottom. This was one hell of a good-looking angel.

In nude splendor, he padded toward what she assumed was a bathroom, only to freeze mid-step. A muscle on the side of his face twitched and he turned toward her. This time the sharp inhale did come. To her horror, Rachel's fascinated gaze plummeted to the spot between his legs.

"Wow." *Crap did I just say that out loud?*

In one quick motion, he put the shorts over his private area, covering what had to be the most alluring male part she'd ever seen. A frown formed and he pinned her with an annoyed look. "How long have you been awake?"

Just long enough. "I'm not sure," Rachel croaked out and averted her eyes to a spot past his shoulder.

"Give me a minute." He continued into the next room.

Rachel sat up and immediately everything began to spin. "Oh, God." She fell back against the pillows and closed her eyes.

"What's wrong?" Just that quick, he was back beside her. With one hand he cupped her face and with the other he peeled back each eyelid and peered into her eyes. Could his eyes be real? They were so light, almost white, with a luminescent surreal sheen. Silver would be the closest she could come to describing the color. He held up a finger. "Follow my movement."

"Are you a d-doctor?" she stuttered, discomfited by his nearness.

"Something like that," he replied and then took her by the

shoulders. "This time move slower." He helped her to a sitting position with unexpected gentleness.

"What happened to me?" She feared his answer.

"You were attacked by a dark Fae, a demon would be more understandable to you," he responded without hesitation.

Damn it, why had she asked? "Did you kill it?"

He nodded and his eyes shifted down, but then continued. "I'm a slayer."

Of course he was. What the hell, demons existed, so why not slayers? Unable to stop it, she giggled. The demon slayer cocked an eyebrow and pinned her with a questioning gaze.

The man was gorgeous. *Concentrate Rachel.* "Err...so what is your name?"

"Roderick."

Under his scrutiny, she fumbled with the blankets. "How long have I been out of it?"

"Three days." Standing back to his impressive height, he declared "you lost a lot of blood; I had to give you a transfusion. I'm afraid you'll have to remain in bed another couple of days, the demon took too much blood and I wasn't able to give you as much as you need."

She eyed the IV bag attached to her arm. "Where did you get blood?"

"I gave you mine." He placed a large hand on her shoulder. "Get some rest, we'll talk later."

"No, I can't stay, I have to go, I'm better...I promise." The last words slurred and her eyes began to droop. "On second thought maybe I will take a short nap."

CHAPTER THREE

TWO DAYS LATER, the knife fell from his hand, clattering onto the kitchen counter. Roderick held onto the edge of the counter as the latest dizzy spell struck.

Cyn, his roommate and fellow slayer, entered the house through the side door eyeing the sandwich he'd made for Rachel. "Hey man, you okay?"

"She's up," he replied and looked at his friend. "How the hell do I know that?"

Cyn leaned against the counter, picked up half the sandwich and took a bite ignoring Roderick's scowl. "You are the local genius so I shouldn't have to explain this, but since your brain seems to be on vacay, I'll break the obvious to you." Cyn took another bite and lifted an eyebrow at him. "You and beauty in there are probably bonded now since you shared your immortal blood with her. Congratulations man, you've got a mate." The lilt of his Scottish accent didn't soften the blow.

"Oh shit."

"Ah, from your sudden lack of color, I'm going to guess the possibility of it happening flew out the window at the presence of the long-legged-super-model-looking chick." His roommate picked up the rest of the sandwich and swaggered toward his own room on the opposite side of the house. He stopped walking. "Uh, you better talk to her, seems like the bond is already in place. Oh, and she's gonna want to ravish all of your body. Mating call and all that," he called over his shoulder. Laughter followed by a slamming door made it obvious Cyn was not going to be of any help. Loud music boomed from inside the room a moment later confirmed it.

Roderick made another sandwich, filled a glass with juice and went to his bedroom. Time to face the consequences of his actions.

Upon entering his bedroom, Rachel emerged from the steamy bathroom wearing one of his t-shirts that barely fell to mid thigh. He almost dropped the plate when her gaze slammed into him. At the same time her tongue darted out and wet her upper lip. Roderick froze, his eyes locked on her mouth. Did she have any idea what that did to him?

"I feel strange. What's happening to me?" Her voice was husky. Gaze not leaving his, she neared. Her blue eyes searched his face for answers while tentative fingers reached up to his face, the soft touch on his jaw made his breath hitch. "You feel it too don't you?"

Unable to look away, a wave of heat hit him and Roderick opened his mouth to warn her to step away. No words came so he simply nodded.

Instead of moving away, she wrapped her arms around his waist and placed her head on his chest. "I need...you to touch me, be with me." Her slender body trembled against his.

"I made a sandwich." He was embarrassed by the huskiness in his own voice.

"Mmmm?" She stood on her tiptoes and began to nibble at his throat.

"Uh, okay, so you're not hungry...let me put this down." He started to turn away only to remain rooted to the spot and letting out groan when she bit into his sensitive skin.

Her hot tongue licked the spot where she'd nipped and Roderick swallowed. "Oh yeah...I mean...no...we need to talk." He gritted out the last word as her hips jutted forward and gyrated into him, her hands firmly grasping his butt.

While he stood there like the damn statue in Midnight in the Garden of Good and Evil, with a plate in one hand and a glass of juice in the other; the woman took full advantage to explore his body.

Her hands swept up from his buttocks to his back and around his neck. She pulled his face down to bring his mouth against hers. At her soft whimper, he responded by kissing her back, the strength of their bond proving greater than his will.

He had to warn her. Rachel needed to know what had happened, sex between them would in all probability cement their bond. Her tongue pushed into his mouth and he was powerless to stop her. The blood bond's tie dragged him into waters too deep to survive.

When her hand wandered between his legs and firm fingers curved over his hardness, the dishes clattered to the carpet. With a growl of surrender, he scooped her up and raced to the bed falling onto it with her. He had to have her.

Nothing else mattered. His blood rushing to the one spot between his legs gave him no option.

Rachel began tearing at his clothes and jerked the t-shirt off over his head, the entire time managing to keep her legs wrapped around his waist.

Working past his shaking hands and her limbs draped about him, Roderick somehow was able to yank his jeans off and remove the t-shirt she wore.

A combination of urge and passion fell over them sending them down a spiral of no return.

"Please!" Rachel screamed and tugged at his hips.

If his life depended on it, there was no way he could deny her. Between kisses, he tried to talk. "You are not in a position to consent to this. This is not what we should be doing." She shoved her tongue into his mouth and he suckled at it for a moment trying to ignore her rubbing against his most sensitive area.

Breaking the kiss, he shoved his face next to hers. "Listen to me. Look at me."

She looked at him, meeting his gaze. "It's a one time thing. I want you, you want me. What's the big deal?"

"It made sense. They had been attracted to one another from the first. It wasn't as if they were teenagers. Adults had one night…er afternoon trysts all the time…"

While he fucking pondered the ins and outs of casual sex, Rachel took his dick, lifted her hips and took him in fully.

"Ah!" He was sure his eyes rolled back into his head. Damn she felt perfect.

He pushed into her hard and fast while she arched, pressing him to delve even deeper. The urgency of their need all-consuming, nothing mattered more than joining as one.

Blood pounded through his veins, he was so hard it was almost painful. From somewhere inside himself, Roderick drew the strength and pulled out. Although the woman was more than ready he didn't want to go all beast on her. She was special, not just beautiful.

Running his hands down her silken skin, he would call her flawless. With perfectly shaped breasts high on her chest, a slender waist and long well formed legs; Rachel could easily enthrall a man. Her lips were parted and her eyes glazed over as he ran his hand between her legs. Using his thumb pad, he circled her center while pushing his finger into her. She was more than ready, her hand covered his and she pushed her hips up to take more.

Once again he thrust in. The urgency of their need all-consuming, nothing mattered more than joining as one.

Her moans turned into cries when they continued. He had to stop, talk to her, explain something, what he wasn't quite sure at the moment. Roderick's entire body began to shake as he attempted to control the instinct to finish.

Lips parted, her mouth was irresistible. He covered it with his and Rachel sucked hard on his tongue when he pushed it into her delicious mouth.

"Holy shit," he couldn't stop the words, his entire body shook so hard, it took all his energy to straighten his arms and push his hips forward. She wrapped her legs around his waist, the position taking him into her entirely.

"Ah!" Rachel raked her nails down his back and threw her head back extending her neck. The fast pulse at her throat took his attention but he turned away and once again took her mouth.

When she grabbed his ass and urged him to move faster, Roderick slid his hands under her and lifted her hips off the bed. He rose to his knees and thrust harder and faster. The sounds of skin slapping against skin became almost as loud as her cries.

"Oh God!" Rachel called out and her sex quivered around his hardness sending him to lose his breath. She went still.

He thrust in twice more, barely able to keep from passing out. When he came, it was so hard he let out a cross between a howl and a moan.

Then he did what he'd been afraid off. He blacked out.

RODERICK'S EYES POPPED open; he looked around the familiar room. Had he dreamed the entire thing? It was then he realized there was someone under him. He rolled off and cradled her against him. Lying on his side, he studied the sleeping beauty. She was still out, but from the soft sigh, not in distress.

"Oh my god, what just happened? Did I black out?" she purred a few minutes later. Her fingers danced up and down his chest. "That was the most incredible sex I've ever had."

Oh yeah, it had been incredible. It had also been incredibly, utterly, unbelievably stupid.

Roderick rolled onto his back and pulled Rachel over onto his chest. He had to talk to her. What would he say? How to tell her life as she'd known it was completely gone. Everything she'd known was changed forever.

Beautiful blue eyes met his, her lips pressed tight and her brow crinkled. "We just had unprotected sex."

"You don't have anything to worry about." He pressed a kiss to her creased brow. "Are you sorry this happened?" Somehow he had to work the conversation into telling her they were now bonded for life.

Her lips curved into a mischievous smirk. "In truth, although I'm not a one night stand kind of woman, I would have kicked myself if I wouldn't have been with you before I left. I don't think I've ever met a hotter guy." She shrugged and snuggled closer. "Are you?"

He let out a breath he wasn't aware he was holding. "You think I'm hot?"

She rolled her eyes at him. "Ah yeah, and I'm sure I'm not the first woman to tell you that." Rachel kissed his jaw, her lips lingering. "The hottest guy I've ever seen." She drew a circle on his chest with her forefinger. "Unforgettably hot."

Crap he was hard again. *Not now. Talk first. Tell her everything.* Not that they had any choice of remaining together. Separation from a bonded mate was not an option, it was not only physically painful, but the need to connect would become all-consuming if they were separated for too long, especially when the connection was new.

"We need to talk," Roderick began. "We have something

special here and I need to explain…" his thoughts faded as Rachel drew herself against his body and began to kiss him again.

"EXPLAIN THIS TO me again? Because you gave me your blood, I'm immortal now?" just as expected as soon as he began to explain the situation, Rachel was no longer curled beside him. Instead she paced in front of the bed, his t-shirt back on. His gaze followed her, roaming over the woman's enticing figure. She was lovely, tall and sinewy but rounded in the right places. Her long golden chestnut hair fell almost to her waist was a tussled mess thanks to his fingers.

His mate. Well, he'd definitely lucked out in the looks department; she was gorgeous.

"Are you listening to me?"

Ah, not really. "I didn't think about the consequences. I took an oath when I became a doctor to save lives when possible. I couldn't leave you to die. I had to do something, anything, to ensure you a chance at survival. It wasn't until my roommate brought it up that I realized the full impact of giving you my blood."

Finally she moved closer, but far enough he couldn't reach her and sat at the foot of the bed. Her curious eyes studied him. "What exactly are you?"

"I am an immortal, part of a group of men known as the

Protectors. Cyn, my roommate is one too. Our sole purpose is to defend innocents from beings that kill. Like the one that attacked you."

Other than a slight widening of her eyes, she seemed to take the news well. "Were you born this way?"

"No," He shook his head. "We are predestined. Chosen by I don't know whom. At about age twenty or so, I began to change. My vision became sharper, hearing keener, and I grew almost a foot and bulked up. The pains were excruciating, the nightmares terrifying. It was during this time our leader, Julian, came to me and explained what happened and why."

When Rachel began to shake, Roderick couldn't stop himself from pulling her into his arms and smoothing her hair.

"How old are you?" she asked against his chest.

"I'm not sure. I was born around 300 AD in Sparta."

Eyebrows lifted, her tempting lips formed an O. "Holy crap! A Spartan, I've read about your kind. The fact your race were known warriors, I can understand why you were chosen." She reached for his hair, her fingers combing through the strands. "Is that why your hair is so blond? Its almost silver."

"No, my hair has always been this color."

He pulled his mate tighter against him and cleared his throat. "There's more you need to know."

His woman was brave by the fortifying breath she took and prepared for whatever he would say next. She pushed back and once again put distance between them. She leaned against his dresser, her arms crossed. "Explain it to me. Am I immortal?"

"You may or may not be. But I would venture to guess my blood will insure your life is prolonged. I am not sure as we are forbidden from giving our blood to humans…mortals."

"So you broke some kind of law for me?"

He closed his eyes for the moment, not wanting to think of Julian's reaction to the news. The Roman was not exactly a nice guy on the best of days. "Yes."

"What else?"

"We are bonded. Mated. Tied to one another."

It was easy to see the wheels turning as her expressions changed from questioning, to 'oh shit' and finally to 'oh hell no'. Intelligence was evident from the fact she reacted by asking another question and not exploding. "Can it be broken?"

He shrugged and clenched his hands. Talk was not what he wanted to do at the moment. Her scent filled his every sense. He itched to touch her, to have her once again. The last thing he expected after so many years of existence was to bond, to be responsible for a female. His life was not easy. Waking each morning more of a gift than a given. Then there was the matter of Julian's reaction to the situation.

He looked to the ceiling only to snap back to Rachel when she let out a huff. "Well, can it?"

"I don't think so. Julian would know. I doubt it. We are tied for life."

She didn't hold back this time. "The hell you say. I choose who I marry and when. I am not like you, it's not going to happen buddy." Her fiery stare met his as she flung her hand between them. "Not happening."

Instead of replying he fell back onto the bed and put his hands behind his head, attention on the whirling ceiling fan. "It's not like I planned it. So you're not the only one stuck."

She loomed over him, her bright eyes meeting his. "Aren't you going to do something?"

"Yeah, but I have to plan what to do, think it through."

Her gaze traveled from his eyes to his mouth and finally to his very obvious desire and she let out a gasp and swallowed. "Shit."

"I know."

"Will it always feel this strong? This need is crazy." Rachel let her mouth fall open and she squeezed her legs together. "I can't allow it to take control."

Roderick reached for her hand and brought it to his lips. "Come to bed. It will only get worse if we resist."

"Damn it," she exclaimed, "I really need to go."

She climbed over him and straddled his waist, her sex flush against his and this time it was Roderick who let out a loud gasp. "Shit."

"One more time, but then I'm leaving."

"Yeah…about that…"

Her hands stopped him from saying anything further as she pushed his shorts low on his hips, grabbed his thickness and guided him inside her.

Talking for the moment had ended.

Finally he managed to get his bearings just as she fell over his chest spent.

Moving slowly, he wrapped his arms around her and held her against him. "It will work out Rachel. I will ensure it."

"I don't know what to say. What to think. I need a few days to process all of this."

"Of course, I understand. I know it feels as if I'm not giving you many options."

She lifted her head and looked at him. "It doesn't just *feel* that way. It is exactly how it is. I have no options, according to you, but to go along with this tradition of yours."

"It's not a tradition. It's a physical reaction to sharing my blood with another." He tried to see it from her perspective. Other than not thinking into what the ramifications of sharing his blood would bring, all he'd concentrated on at the time had been saving her. Of course the situation was easier for him to deal with, he'd been part of this world for a very long time.

One thing was for certain; at the moment he didn't regret the bond.

CHAPTER FOUR

T HE BACK STREETS of Midtown were quiet and full of shadows. There were plenty of places for dark Fae to hide with their unlucky victims. The crunching of gravel under his boots seemed to echo. Yeah so he wasn't being stealthy this night, but whatever. If an idiot was stupid enough to hunt in his territory then he'd at least give him a running start.

And...there it was. The thing darted from behind a dumpster and ran away from where Roderick neared. It sprinted like an Olympian going for the gold only to shriek and skid to a stop when Cyn appeared at the end of the street.

The Scot lifted his chin as if in greeting. "All alone tonight? Kill your date or something?"

The demon growled and yanked out a handgun. It cranked his head to Roderick and then back to Cyn. "Let me by. I'll shoot you in the head. Even you cannot survive that."

Cyn rolled his eyes and lifted a brow at the demon. "Seriously? I doubt you're that good of a shot demon."

The gun blast echoed. Only seconds later after a swift slash of his sword, the demon's head rolled onto the ground. Cyn was looking behind him to ensure no one was shot while both the body and head evaporated, a thick blue smoke spreading over the ground like a mist.

"Well that was boring," Cyn said waiting for Roderick to sheath his sword. "What about the victim?"

"Homeless man. Dead." Roderick stalked to the sidewalk and let out a breath.

"Bummer...get it? Bum...mer."

"A man is dead. Do you ever take anything serious?"

His friend seemed to ponder. "Nope."

Cynden Fraser was young at only two hundred and twenty-five, not yet tired of the continuous circle of killing demons only for them to multiply.

The never-ending war between the Protectors and dark forces was rarely with odds in their favor. Roderick longed for a time when they would grow exponentially. Julian had recruited hundreds into their army, but when fighting thousands of evil creatures, it made little difference.

Even though, they were stronger, faster and had the advantage of not having to feed from humans to survive, they were severely outnumbered. He wondered at times what the point of it all was.

"Three o'clock," Cyn muttered watching three men and two women heading to another side street. The women giggled loudly at something one of the males said.

"Dark Fae," Roderick said and picked up the pace. "Lets ruin their party."

They rushed into the darkness then stopped abruptly. Roderick stilled his breath and allowed his keen ears to pick up where the people had gone. "There," he motioned to a door on the side of an industrial looking building. "Cover me."

Careful to not make noise, he pulled the door open and stepped into the darkness. It reeked of a mixture of oil and dampness. The shuffling of a rodent and the wind against the top windows were the only noise until a soft whimper sounded from further inside.

His partner went to the left side and Roderick to the right and they stalked forward. He caught himself smiling. Okay so maybe there was the thrill of the hunt that showed up at times like this. It was like a game of cat and mouse. The only downer in the whole situation was the possibility of victims being hurt or worse.

Shouts sounded and they took advantage of the noise to race to a side room. They pushed the door open and stepped in.

It must have been an office at one time, but it seemed the demons had gone all Martha Steward and fixed it up to look like a bedroom, curtains included.

Five sets of eyes looked to the door. The demons hissed and snarled and one of the women fainted. She slid down the wall, flopping onto the floor. Both women were nude. Obviously they'd been led to believe it was going to be an orgy. Perhaps after they'd fucked and fed, the demons planned to keep them alive for a bit. Sooner or later, they'd kill the women. It wasn't wise to leave witnesses to their existence.

Two of the three demons flew at the Protectors, knives in hand. The one that attacked Roderick held two long wicked looking knives. He sliced across the air over and over. "You'll be chopped up in little pieces by the time I'm done." He slashed again. "We'll finish our party while you lay on the ground bleeding." He stepped closer and attempted to stab him. "I'm going to fuck you up…"

The demon's head plopped onto the floor with a sickening thud and the other woman shrieked so loud his ears rang. The remaining male had escaped out through a window while he and Chatty Cathy had gone on and on. Cyn had gone after him and Roderick remained in the room with the nude women.

"Get dressed," he told the one who continued to whimper. "Help me get some clothes on your friend." He bent to the woman who'd passed out. She'd been bitten, but from the looks of it the demon had only commenced to feed.

"Am I going to turn into a vampire?" The other woman asked as she scrambled into her dress. "Oh my God. I don't want to become something like that."

"You won't." He tugged a t-shirt onto the limp woman.

When Cyn came back a few moments later both women sat on the bed and stared at him. The one who'd fainted was obviously drunk. "He's hot," she told no one in particular, then glanced to Roderick. "You're hot too."

Roderick looked at Cyn. "Scrub their mind. I'm going to scout and make sure no one else was coming to join the festivities."

The street was deserted. Not quiet as the sounds of passing cars and voices of people on the busier street in front of the building floated in the air.

Seconds later the women came out from the building, gave him a curious look and scrambled to the sidewalk. He walked behind them and watched until they melded with others on the sidewalk.

When Cyn walked out, Roderick turned to his partner. "What did you say to them? They gave me a strange look."

"Just that the only other person in the room was a tall blond man who had no pecker."

Roderick gave Cyn a droll look. "I'm serious."

"So am I." The guy walked off whistling.

"You're an asshole." Roderick let out a breath. If he killed his partner, he'd be paired off with either Thor, the Viking who was about as subtle as a category five tornado, or the Rowe who gave him the creeps. The guy never talked and moved so silently even other Protectors lost him.

"Wait up. Let's go grab a bite."

Cynden always hungry stopped mid-stride. "Good idea."

They settled into a booth in an all night diner. Cyn squirted ketchup into his mouth. "I'm starving."

It was almost one in the morning and soon the place would be filled with clubbers. As much as he hated being seen out in leathers and a sword across his back, he couldn't help the rumble in his stomach. Lately he was always hungry.

"You need to get laid more. Not like you to take so many meal breaks."

"I get laid enough," he grunted not wanting to discuss Rachel with Cyn. "More than you." He added with a raised eyebrow just to egg his partner on.

Cyn shrugged. "I'm not bonded, so I can go without longer. Not that I enjoy doing the left hand gig, but whatever. Women are not worth the trouble."

That was a true statement. Most women were not worth it. But when he thought of Rachel, he could not picture his life without her. She was beautiful, giving and in bed, they were like...

"Dude you're smiling." Cyn leaned across the table and snapped his fingers in front of Roderick's face. "What you want to order?"

It was then he noticed a server stood beside the table staring at him. "Sir, can I take your order?"

"Yeah...a double burger with cheese, two orders of fries and a milkshake."

When the waitress shuffled off, Cyn laughed. "So when does your girl move in? Can I stay or should I start looking for a place?"

"Don't know. And yeah...as much as you annoy me, I'd rather you not move out."

"My heart flutters," Cyn said and squirted more ketchup into his mouth. "You love me...you really love me."

"I'm stuck with you, which is very different."

The server brought their shakes and both delved in. Cyn gave him a quizzical look. "Truth is I hope she comes around soon. She's your other half and I'm happy for you brother."

Shit, now he had to admit he liked the guy.

CHAPTER FIVE

"**H**OW LONG ARE you going to torture the poor man?" said Rachel's mother, Mariam, as she eyed the long stemmed white rose in her hand. Rachel turned away to fill a crystal bud vase and placed the bloom in it before setting it on the counter.

That her mom accepted the news so well of her newly prolonged life and being mated forever to an immortal demon slayer, still amazed her. Perhaps her mother's addiction to paranormal romance finally came in handy. Over time, they'd figure out how to break the news to her father, but for now, they kept the secret between them.

"For two weeks you've kept him at arms length knowing darn well you're in love with him." Her mom arched a knowing brow. "Deny it."

After much cajoling, Rachel had convinced Roderick that her mother would have to know by telling him she could never keep the secret from who she considered her best friend. Besides, there was no way in hell she was going through this alone.

She observed her mother glance at the rose with lips pursed, Mariam would not give up until Rachel married

Roderick. The woman could be relentless. Maybe telling her had been a mistake.

A snappy retort in check, she replied. "I don't like that Roderick didn't give me a choice in this." Her chin jutted out at the hollow words. "He took the choice of who I would spend my life with away from me."

"Roderick sleeps here often." With a sparkle in her eye, Mariam picked up her cup of tea and sipped, her soft blue eyes watching her over the rim. "You're obviously enjoying the relationship."

"Mom! I told you, we have to. As bonded mates it's physically painful not to er...touch regularly." A tingle swept through her as the picture of Roderick under her, his handsome face thrown back while they made love that morning flashed into her mind. Her gaze slid toward her bedroom where he presently slept.

Every morning Roderick brought a token, whether a rose like today, some chocolate or her favorite cappuccino from the nearby café. Not only that, but their chemistry was off the charts. She couldn't deny the handsome man fulfilled her every dream in a partner.

"All right, I admit the basis of my reluctance to accept him fully and to move in together is fear." Rachel said as she flipped absently through a Southern Lady magazine on the kitchen table. "I'm not ready to lose the little bit of control I have left. Mom, you know I'm not a control freak by nature or even close, but it's just this entire scenario takes time to get used to."

Her mother's hand covered hers in understanding.

Roderick proved to be a patient man, other than coming to her bed every morning, he never pressured her to make the decision to live together. She'd never deny him her body. Nor would she chance being the cause of him being hurt or worse. If he fought with the distraction of their bond calling, he could be killed.

Not that she could resist Roderick anyway. By the time he arrived at her home at dawn, her desire for him was so overwhelming she practically took the man in the doorway.

Then there was a new matter she'd not expected, another blow to her already fragile hold on sanity. She suspected she was expecting. How would Roderick react if her suspicion she was pregnant were true?

"Well he's not going to wait forever, honey." Her mother brought her back to the conversation. "If I were you, I'd make up my mind one way or another. It's not fair to either one of you to keep this up if there's no choice anyway is there?" Her mom stood to go. "I better go, I have a tennis match with your dad in half an hour." She paused and smiled at Rachel. "Just think about it. Drag the situation out too long and he'll figure out a way to break this bond thing."

Would he? Her stomach flipped.

FINDING FOUR DEMONS in the midst of a blood bath after they attacked a group of young women out clubbing, changed the direction of their otherwise quiet night on patrol.

Roderick rushed toward the melee his sword in hand. Just as he rounded into the empty lot, Cyn came into view from the opposite direction. One of the women still conscious screamed and fainted. It was for the best, what was about to happen was not meant for human eyes.

Prepared to defend itself, a high-level demon pulled his sword and lunged at him, the blade slicing barely an inch from his throat. While shifting to avoid the sharp edge ascending past his neck once again, Roderick flung a dagger at another demon. The dagger hit its mark and the attacking demon stopped mid-stride and evaporated.

At the next swipe of the persistent demon's sword, Roderick dove to the ground, rolled and flipped back to his feet. The momentum gave him the benefit of surprise, his size and reach adding to the advantage. He cut clean across the shocked demon's neckline. The head landed with a solid thud onto the pavement rolling only a few inches before both it and the body vaporized.

It was his turn to be caught off-guard when a swooshing sound accompanied by a stinging cut to his left shoulder. He slammed his fist into the demon's stomach and cut the low-level down across the chest. The demon fell and faded, the blue mist mixing with the others'. He grabbed at his shoulder to stifle the bleeding.

Damn, he was getting sloppy.

Blades clashed. Roderick swung around to check for other threats, only to find Cyn just killed another demon, the navy haze snaking around the male's Doc Martens. The Protectors' luminescent gaze scanned the area and Cyn held up a peace sign, letting him know it was clear.

They checked the vitals on the victims. One was dead, but the other two would survive. Cyn called the local authorities after they erased the women's memories of the occurrence and gathered up the demons' weapons.

Roderick stalked away from the scene ignoring his partner's slanted look. As expected, Cyn stepped alongside and grabbed his arm swinging him around to face him.

"You almost got waxed. Twice." Cyn didn't release the hold. "What the hell is wrong with you Roderick? This is the first time I've ever seen a demon barely miss cutting your head off—even worse, one of them actually cut you," he continued with a pointed look to the bloodstain seeping through the shirt on his shoulder. The wound was already healing.

Cyn lifted an eyebrow. "It looks like a deep cut. Good thing we heal fast. You okay?"

"I'm good." He shrugged the hand off and took a breath. To make things worse, he was winded. It hadn't even been a real fight.

They'd reached their motorcycles, and Roderick turned to look at his partner. "All right, I'll admit it, maybe I'm a bit distracted. It's this whole mate thing." With hesitation, he met his friend's gaze. "I don't know if I want to be mated. I'm over 1600 years old. If anything I was looking more forward to dying than starting a new life. The stubborn woman refuses to move in with me, which makes it harder to concentrate. This…" He slammed his hand against his skull. "This need to be with her, to see her is almost crippling. I can't stop thinking about Rachel and I don't like it."

"Yeah, I don't envy you." Cyn shook his head. "Julian doesn't even know yet. More fun times ahead."

Great point. He wasn't looking forward to their leader's take on the matter.

His partner lifted both brows. "The Roman must not have found out yet, else he'd be here, bashing your head through a wall for breaking several of the Protectors' basic rules."

"He's the least of my worries right now. Rachel is going to have to make a decision and soon. I don't blame her for what she's feeling, but it's not like it can be changed now."

Sirens wailed in the distance. They rounded their bikes in silence, the sound of their boots crunching on the graveled ground filled the space.

"Maybe you need to take a couple days off and spend time with her. Let her know you can't continue like this...."

The ground under him swayed, everything tilted, something hit him in the face.

Hard.

"Hey Roderick?" Cyn was shaking him.

What the hell? He'd just face-planted onto the gravel surface. Roderick rolled onto his back. Swirls of light swam before him. "What just happened?"

"I think you're going to have to tell Julian. Something is definitely wrong." Cyn helped him get to his feet. "You're damn lucky it didn't happen while we fought."

"You think?"

CHAPTER SIX

RACHEL PACED IN her living room and once again glanced at the wall clock. Roderick was extremely late—which meant she'd be late for work. Good thing the need did not appear to be as strong today. Maybe it was beginning to wane. Picking up the cell phone, she considered maybe the urgency of the bonding was ebbing. He'd explained to her that it would become bearable over time, and they wouldn't need to be together daily. Just thinking about their lovemaking brought the familiar rush of heat, which pooled in all the wrong places.

With the phone cradled against her ear, she headed to her bedroom to get dressed. She wasn't sure what kind of day she'd have at the library today. If Roderick didn't appear, it would be the first day since they'd mated that she'd face without first seeing him. Panic clenched her midsection at hearing his deep voice, the message short. "*Rod's phone—leave a message.*"

"Hi, just wondering if you are all right. Please call me." *I miss you.* She wasn't ready to let him know how strong her feelings for him had become. What if something happened to him? Was he lying in some dark alley dying? What if it was all because of her not moving in with him?

"Oh God." With trembling fingers, she scanned her contacts for Cyn's number.

"Hello?" The Scot's deep timbre did little to settle her nerves.

"I haven't seen Roderick today, he hasn't shown up..." Rachel felt like an overbearing housewife at the words, but she plugged on. "Do you know where he is? Is he all right?"

"Uh, yeah," he hesitated. The cryptic reply made her want to reach through the phone and crush his windpipe. "He's asleep."

"Oh." Rachel wasn't sure what else to say. "Okay. Well I left him a message. Thanks. Bye."

"Hey Rachel." Cyn stopped her from hanging up. "You need to talk to him. He's probably going to punch my face in for telling you this, but he's having a hard time with, err... never mind. You just need to talk to him and the sooner the better."

After calling the library to let them know she was taking a vacation day, Rachel jumped in her blue Honda Civic hatchback and headed to Roderick's house. With Christmas coming up, things were slow at the library. However they were planning several events the following week, so she'd have to work extra hours to make sure all went well.

The hour-long drive to Roderick's house gave her time to think and practice her words. She'd made a decision, she would ask him if he'd rather move into her townhouse, or else she'd move in with him. At the same time Rachel planned to inform him that she wanted to get married. Not that she was old fashioned, but if she was tied to a man for life and possibly having his child, then she wanted a marriage certificate.

THE PROTECTORS LIVED in an oversized log cabin with architectural lines that could easily grace a magazine cover. The imposing, well-built structure gave the impression of easy access, but she knew a complex security system kept track of anyone that neared the home. She pulled into the driveway and stepped out of the car after palming a remote that allowed her entry onto the grounds without setting off the alarms.

The interior of the house was silent when Rachel let herself in with the key that hung on the same ring as the remote.

The muted sound of rock music came from the direction of Cyn's bedroom and she smiled shaking her head. How could the man sleep with music constantly blaring?

Padding to Roderick's bedroom, apprehension swirled around her like a thick fog. He'd not come to her today, had not even called. So...here she was checking in on him. When she reached for the doorknob, Rachel couldn't make herself open the door.

Maybe her mother was right. Not making up her mind to move in together had finally put him off and he was looking for a way to break it off. Was it possible?

Rachel swung around, stalked back to the front room and screamed.

What could only be described as a god stood in the middle of the space. An arched eyebrow was his only response to her shriek. Olive skinned with a muscular yet sleek physique, the man had almost blue-black hair that was combed away from an indescribably handsome face.

"Who are you?" Rachel asked nearing him instead of the smarter move, which would be to get away. "You're one of them aren't you?"

Before he could answer, Roderick and Cyn burst into the room from opposite directions, both holding swords and neither fully dressed. In fact, Roderick wore only boxers and Cyn was completely nude. The men froze at spotting the newcomer. Roderick's eyes widened when noting her presence.

Both men dropped their swords to their sides simultaneously.

"Hello Julian." Cyn was the first to find his voice. The man then had the nerve to cross his arms over his chest and lean on the doorjamb, his eyes darting between the other three people in the room. Rachel tried hard not to stare at his nude physique.

Roderick cleared his throat and dropped his gaze to Cyn's private area. "Do you mind covering your naked ass?"

"And miss what's about to go down? I don't think so." His Scottish accent seemed heavier in his amusement.

"Cyn." Roderick motioned toward Rachel.

The Scot returned a bland stare, but at least he was decent enough to grab a throw and wrap it around his waist before dropping onto the nearest couch.

This was Julian? Their leader? He didn't seem old enough, perhaps twenty-three, twenty-four at the most. Yet when she studied him closer, he seemed more ageless than young.

Julian remained quiet, an aura like that of a panther about to pounce on his prey exuded from him. He didn't look directly at anyone in particular yet seemed to take it all in.

Roderick moved to Rachel's side and placed a protective arm around her waist pulling her not just to him, but also slightly behind his side. "I can explain…"

A muscle twitched along Julian's jawline and his furious gaze slammed into them. In the next instant Roderick flew across the room, and crashed into the opposite wall.

Rachel shrieked.

Before he could fall to the floor, he was thrown again, this time bouncing off the fireplace wall before crumpling onto the floor. Bricks from the hearth surrounded him as he struggled to his feet only to be flung back against the first wall and held there by some invisible force. Roderick seemed to struggle to breath and Rachel rushed at Julian.

"Stop it!" She hit the Roman in the chest. "Leave him alone."

Julian didn't even flinch. Roderick continued to flail and struggle when Julian's black gaze jerked to her. "This is Protector business, go wait in another room."

"Like hell!" Rachel kneed him in the groin, satisfied when he grunted and doubled over. At the same time Roderick collapsed to the floor and she raced to him. His glazed eyes met hers for only a moment before he jumped to his feet, grabbed Rachel by the arm and threw her behind him, his trembling body blocking her view of the asshole Julian.

"Get her out of the room Cynden." Julian's soft Italian-accented command laced with rage gave Rachel goose bumps.

"I'm not leaving." She peeked around Roderick to glare at the man. "You are crazy if you think I'm going to wait in the next room while you kill him." She swung toward Cyn. "And you, why don't you do something?"

Julian didn't speak, instead his gaze met Roderick's. They were communicating telepathically, she didn't know how she knew this, but her suspicions were confirmed when Roderick grunted and nodded in response.

"He's not going to kill me Rachel. Go on, wait in the bedroom. I need to talk to him."

Rachel didn't budge until Roderick took her by the elbow and walked her towards the doorway. His beautiful silver eyes were clear again when they met hers. "You'll only make things worse for me by not doing what he asks. Please just go and wait. I'll be all right, he won't kill me."

"Without even touching you, he just beat the crap out of you!" Her voice rose as she dared another glare at Julian. "How can you be sure he won't murder you?"

Roderick had the nerve to smile. "I've known Julian for decades. He's just angry."

Pushing Roderick's arm aside, she glared at Julian one last time. "You need anger management classes," she huffed and stomped to his bedroom.

The soft click assured him that Rachel was out of earshot. Roderick swung back to Julian purposely ignoring the throbs of protest from his bruised body. "You didn't have to do that. I was prepared to speak to you."

"Is that so?" Julian sneered, his piercing gaze searing. "I seriously doubt you were in a hurry to travel to Rome and inform me of your blatant disregard for our laws."

"He didn't plan for this to ha—" Cyn stopped talking when Julian snarled.

"How long?"

The abstract question took Roderick by surprise. Mentally, he scrambled to figure out the exact timetable since he and Rachel bonded. "Sixteen days, give or take a day."

Julian paced, his hands gripped behind his back. In all the decades he'd known Julian, this was the first time his leader had disciplined him. What could be so bad that Julian seemed at a loss for words? When the Roman finally turned to him, Roderick held his breath.

"A blood-bond is normally unbreakable." He stated the obvious. "Fortunately, you did not bond correctly. Our rules are there for a purpose Roderick. There's a reason why you are not allowed to mate unless the woman is the right one. It has to be a life mate or it will drain you of your powers, your immortality." Julian turned, his eyes locked on his. "You must give her up. And you will leave the Protector Force."

Roderick's mouth fell open. "Are you saying our bonding can be broken? Why do I have to resign as a Protector?" The thumping of his heartbeat thundered in his ears. The only life he'd ever known was slipping from his fingers and he'd yet to understand what Julian expected.

"When a Protector bonds with someone who is not a life

mate, his powers can diminish. You were not just asleep when I arrived, but passed out. The combination of fighting and having to be with her daily is taking its toll on you."

"That sucks," Cyn mumbled under his breath.

The chair Roderick slumped into groaned under his weight. Julian was right. He was fatigued, barely able to get home every day after leaving Rachel's house. Today he'd not even had the energy to ride to her place. After passing out in the street, he'd never felt so drained and it had frightened him. Once home, his weighty limbs had barely allowed him to make it from the shower to the bed before he collapsed onto it. "What's happening to me?"

Julian's gaze softened. He neared and placed a hand on Roderick's shoulder. Energy surged through him, electric tingles raced up his legs through his chest. When Julian pulled his hand away, Roderick jumped to his feet. Every ache and pain was gone, his entire body restored.

"It's temporary, perhaps a week or two before your energy will begin to wane again. I would suggest you maintain your distance from her, but the need will become impossible to resist."

"Can the bond be broken?"

"Not at the moment."

"Does this mean I can remain a Protector?"

"No." The reply was clear.

"Damn it Julian, help me out here. What am I supposed to do? If I can't break the bond, how the hell am I supposed to get rid of her? I don't want to quit. Being a Protector is my life."

A gasp made them all turn to the doorway. Rachel stood with her hand to her throat. By her stricken expression, she'd overheard his ranting. Without a word, she turned on her heel and raced from the room.

Recovering late, Roderick ran after her, catching up just as she reached her car. He grabbed her arm. An ache tore through his chest at seeing tears pouring down her face.

She tried to yank her arm from his grip. "Let me go. I don't want to be here, I have to get away from you and him." She motioned toward the house with her other hand. "I didn't ask for any of this. I thought…I am stupid enough to care for you. All these days of trying to convince me this was more than just a physical thing, you're yelling at the top of your lungs how you want to get rid of me." Rachel gulped for air and tried to jerk her arm free again. "Let me go Rod, please."

"I can't let you drive like this. You're too upset." He reached for her but she inched away. "Look I'm upset too, I didn't expect Julian. I didn't mean it the way it sounded. Hell, I'm confused by all this and not sure what to do." He attempted to pull her toward the house. "Please come back inside. Let's decide together what we need to do."

"No." Rachel shook her head and placed her hand over her mouth, fresh tears springing to her eyes. "I don't want to face him again, not right now. Go back inside Rod, talk it out, figure out how we can break this bond so you can *get rid of me* and I can go on with my life," she said emphasizing the words he'd said earlier.

Hands on his chest, she pushed him away. "I'm fine to

drive, I really need to get away from you. I'm going home."

Reluctantly, he released her arm. "I will come to your house later."

Her shiny tear-filled gaze met his and they maintained the contact for a beat before Rachel turned away and slid into the car.

Her driving seemed to be under control, the vehicle glided away and Roderick raked a hand down his face. He was such an ass. He'd made her cry. Damn Julian for his rotten timing.

Had she just said she cared for him? His chest tightened.

"I'm not going to break the bond, so just tell me what I need to do." Roderick stalked into the living room and stopped short. Julian was gone.

Cyn remained on the couch, the throw barely covering his midsection. He pointed at a wooden box on the floor next to the fireplace. "Julian left something for you. He said once you make the decision he wants to see you in Rome."

"Damn it." Roderick ignored the item and sank into a chair. "What the hell did he accomplish by coming here? Rachel is upset and offended. I'm confused and you're still naked."

"He energized you, that's a good thing." The Scot scowled and shook his head. "Did you just say you're not going to break the bond? Damn, you're in love. It's sad to witness the fall of Roderick the Great." Cyn's eyes flickered to the box. "Aren't you going to see what's in there?"

"Describe it." Roderick asked.

"What?" Cyn's brow crinkled. "Describe what?"

"Love."

His roommate shrugged and looked away in thought. "I think it's like a thorn or a splinter. Something that gets under your skin and it's hard as hell to get out. No matter how deep you dig for it, you can't get it out." At his pained expression Cyn's brows lifted. "That might be a bad example. Hell, I don't know. I've been close to it once, and from what I remember it mostly turns you into a wuss."

Great, now he was even further confused. Roderick pulled on sweatpants and headed to the garage. He rolled his red Ducati Monster onto a cement pad behind it and lowered the kickstand on the motorcycle. It didn't really need washing, but he needed something to do so he pulled out a bucket, sponge and a water hose, the entire time deep in thought. Was it possible he felt more than attraction for Rachel?

Spartans were not an emotional people. He barely remembered his parents ever in the same room with him as a child.

His mother was a gruff woman, her curt commands to him and his siblings the normal way. One afternoon, after cutting his hand open, he'd run inside his home to find her. With his father off to battle, he'd not thought to find another man lying with his mother. She hadn't bothered to cover up their nudity, instead had told him to go find his older sister to clean up the wound.

That was the way of Spartans, it seemed, for when he'd run and told his sister, she'd shrugged it off as if it were normal. Once he was old enough to go to battle, he learned most Spartans did not expect fidelity from the women left behind.

They sure as hell didn't waste time seeking sexual pleasure from other women or men themselves.

He'd left home before having the chance to marry, Julian finding him when he'd barely begun the change and had only been with one woman.

Over the years, lovers came and went but he'd never given any relationship an opportunity for more than a passing liaison.

Roderick finished the chore and put everything away in the garage.

Maybe he'd call the only mated Protector he knew, Joaquin, a Spaniard. The Protector seemed content when he'd last seen him. That's what he'd do… call Joaquin and ask him if he was in love.

Was that what he felt for Rachel? When did his feelings end and the blood-bond begin?

He looked at his watch; it was getting late and he needed to shower and dress. Mostly he needed Rachel. The thought of her brought a smile and lightness in his chest.

"Well I'll be damned, maybe I am in love."

CHAPTER SEVEN

T HE WOMAN IN the mirror had hollow eyes. They reflected hurt and emptiness that could only come from a broken heart. Rachel swiped away the steam that formed and continued to stare at her reflection.

"What am I going to do now?" The wide toothed comb caught in her wet hair and she tugged at it without gentleness. It was a wonder there was any steam in there at all. She'd taken a tepid shower in hopes of cooling her body from the need to be with him. Roderick would be there any minute and she needed to maintain her distance, if not physically, emotionally.

She donned a robe and padded to the bedroom.

If what Julian said was true, there might be a way to break the bond. She would insist they break it and each of them go on with their life as if nothing ever happened between them.

It would be much easier for Roderick. He didn't love her.

Moving forward was something she could do, but to forget him would be impossible. Her hand slid to her still flat stomach and her gaze jerked to the trashcan.

The test she'd picked up on her way home came up positive. She was pregnant.

Single parenting was not exactly in her plans, but that

didn't matter. She'd have her child and would love it so much that having one parent would be more than enough. The dinging of the doorbell pulled her to the present. Roderick didn't use his key today, which meant he was already disengaging.

There was no need to dress. It was inevitable they'd have sex. At the knowledge, her body responded with a heated rush. Rachel steeled her heart and opened the door.

In one fluid motion, Roderick entered and wrapped his arms around her. Crushed against his chest, Rachel struggled to push back. Somehow his hold was firm and gentle at the same time, not allowing for her to move away.

"I forgot my key. Rachel, I'm so sorry," Roderick whispered against her hair. "Please forgive me for those stupid words." He cupped her chin lifting her face to his. "I'm sorry for making you cry. It wasn't my intention…"

"Don't say anymore!" Rachel screamed and shoved at his chest. Still, he did not release her, so she slumped in resignation. "Rod, I don't hold it against you. I understand you aren't happy at being forcibly tied to me. What hurts is you lied to me. You led me to believe you were invested emotionally."

"I…" he stopped speaking and released her. "You're right." His words cut a new hole in her heart. "Being bonded was something I never considered, especially after living for so many centuries." He looked up at the ceiling in thought.

Rachel backed further away. Every word he spoke struck like a dagger to her soul.

"Call Julian, let him know we need to know how to break

the bond. Whatever I need to do, I will do it." She was relieved no tears fell so she continued. "Just don't say anything else, please."

"I don't want to break the damn bond," Roderick moved so fast, she didn't have time to react. His mouth crushed hers with so much need it shocked her. Tears sprang to her eyes. How could she live without this? Her Protector no longer a part of her life?

With swift motions, Roderick picked her up and took the familiar path to her bedroom. He set her on her feet and pulled the belt of her robe, sliding the garment off her shoulders so it pooled around her feet. When he backed up, his gaze roamed over her sending a delicious tingle. Maintaining eye contact, he began to undress and Rachel mentally devoured every inch the fabric slid off of.

His beautiful silver gaze on her, a slight curve to his sensuous lips. It was impossible to look away as he pulled his shirt off. Within seconds he stood before her, fully nude and all man.

When he stalked to the bed, the only sound she could formulate was a sharp inhalation.

They landed in the bed, a tangle of arms and legs, each vying to touch more of the other's body with a desperation like that of lovers separated for too long.

His mouth took hers as she raked her fingers into his hair holding him in place.

"Now," she cried out…"please."

The erotic sounds of his hard breathing in her ear took her

attention as he guided his hardness to her center. Finally he pushed in. Inch by inch, he moved with excruciating slowness. Incredible how the simple act made her tremble all over. She licked his throat, tracing circles on the soft skin knowing he enjoyed it.

It was easy to lose herself in the friction of each movement as he moved in and out of her. Rachel clung to his broad shoulders as he picked up the pace. Perfect and all consuming, every stroke sent her closer to the brink, the edge she couldn't wait to fall over.

By the time he found the energy to roll off of her, Rachel was finally able to form a coherent thought. She scooted away from him. She not only needed space, but had to protect her heart.

"Why are you laying so far from me?" Roderick lay on his side, his luminescent eyes scouring her face for answers. "I don't want to break the bond Rachel. I choose to stay with you."

"Can you still be a Protector?"

"No. Mated or not, he's punishing me by cutting me loose. I will speak with Julian to see if perhaps he will reconsider, but I doubt it. He rarely changes his mind once he makes a decision. Actually, I don't think he's ever changed his mind."

Rachel rolled to her side facing him. "Then we must go to Italy and see him. We'll ask him to break the bond. There is no need to remain bonded."

"You don't want to be bonded to me?" The soft question shook her. Was he hurt? Or was it just his ego?

"I don't want you to lose your job because of me."

With a growl, Roderick got out of the bed and began to yank his clothes on. "I have to go to work. I have another week until my replacement arrives. Hopefully I will be able to last that long without losing all my energy. Then I'll to go to Rome and meet with Julian." An emotion flickered across his face when he looked at her, but she couldn't decipher what it was. "Know one thing Rachel. We are not breaking up."

She ignored the tug of the words at her heartstrings. "What's happening to you?" Rachel asked reaching for his arm. "Why are you becoming weak?"

He sat on the edge of the bed to pull on his boots. "When a Protector shares his blood, he also shares his immortality. When it's done wrong, the Protector is at risk. The keener eyesight, hearing and night vision, coupled with the need to forge the bond all come together and drain too much energy from my body. Julian left some stuff behind for me to sort through, one of the items is a mating set we can use in an effort to form a proper bond. If it works then I should be able to gain back my ability to stay strong."

"And if it doesn't?" Guilt twisted around her gut. He'd lost it all because he'd saved her life.

"Then I will be a regular guy, who lives a long time, I suppose. It's one of the things I need to talk to Julian about."

He reached for her and kissed her, the softness in the action touched her to the core, but she reminded herself not once had Roderick said he cared for her.

A soft smile curved his lips. "Don't worry, it will be fine.

I'm a doctor, I have a PhD, I can get a job easy." He snapped his fingers. "Just have to figure out how to mask my eyes. Contacts I suppose." With a casual shrug, meant to ease her worry, he stood and stretched. "Gotta go. I'll see you tomorrow all right?"

"Roderick?"

He stopped in the doorway and turned. Rachel's heart hammered in her chest with newfound appreciation. The man was gorgeous. Although huge, he was well formed, somehow muscular without being too bulky. His long silver hair, tussled after their lovemaking, was now pulled back with a thin leather strap that showcased his strong jawline. She absorbed his features from his patrician nose to his well-formed legs.

"Please be careful."

EVEN WITH THE upcoming meeting, Rachel couldn't help but be affected by the beauty of the Italian countryside. The winding road from the larger city of Rome to the town of Olgiata cut through stunning landscape. Villas and tall thin pine-like trees dotted the sides of the road. Once, when everything settled and her life became more stable, she vowed to return and spend time exploring the wonderful country. For now, her focus was on one thing and for that she had to be prepared. There were no assurances, no idea whatsoever in her mind as to what would happen in the next moments. But she had to try; it was time for someone to stand up to the Roman.

Julian's picturesque villa took her breath away. Although she'd been to beautiful homes before, she'd never seen a house so gorgeous. None of the Protectors seemed to be hurting for money.

A doorman of sorts answered the door and showed Rachel inside into an open red-tiled expanse that made up a combination living room and open terrace. Her heels clicked on the tile when she walked across the airy space. She noted most of his furnishings were white. The home was not quite austere, but not inviting either.

The view from the terrace beckoned and Rachel went out to admire the landscape. She grasped the banister while leaning over to take it all in. "Beautiful."

"Welcome Rachel." Julian's deep voice flooded over her like ice water and instantly her heartbeat quickened. She swung to see him stride toward her. Barefoot, wearing jeans and a t-shirt, he seemed at ease in the space. His movements, although graceful, put her on edge.

"Please join me for a glass of Chianti." He stopped next to an ornate marble-topped sideboard of sorts and poured two glasses of wine, his eyes constantly lifting to her face.

Julian joined her at the terrace and although he didn't stand too close, Rachel had to force herself not to put more distance between them when she took the proffered glass from his hand.

The Roman looked away, seeming to study the panorama, and Rachel took advantage of his distraction to study him.

Julian reminded her of a masterpiece. Beautiful yet untouchable. Impenetrable walls surrounded him, the invisible force field emanating an energy that terrified her.

"Are you not thirsty?" The cock of his eyebrow at the still full glass in her hand almost made her drop it. *He knew.*

"I-I am here to speak to you about Rod...Roderick." Rachel stuttered, setting the wineglass none-to-gently on the thick banister. "Please break our bond and allow him to fight in your Protector force again. It all happened because he saved my life. How could you punish him for that?"

Julian looked away again. "I have known the Spartan for a long time. Do you know when I found him, he lay dying in the middle of a battlefield? He was the only survivor of a clash against Messenian forces. His flesh shredded by spears, his bones smashed into the ground under the warhorses' hooves of the departing Slavonic army. Yet he lived. Crazed with pain, he somehow hung on. He was amazing, relentless, a true male of worth." The Roman's penetrating gaze met hers. "The reason he lived is his strong will, Rachel."

"Even more of a reason why you need him," Rachel pleaded.

The man regarded her without expression. It was as if she spoke to a granite statue. "I will not change my mind about this. You've wasted your time and money coming here."

"Why?" Rachel screamed. "This is crazy. Rod told me they are already outnumbered in Atlanta, and you're going to take him off the streets because of an understandable mistake? I'm willing to break the bond with him. Please do it, break us apart and allow him to go back to work."

The floor shook beneath her feet and Rachel shrieked in fear. Jaw clenched, Julian's angry eyes bore into her and he took her forearm, his fingers digging into her skin. "You know nothing little girl. Do you think I make decisions idly? Roderick is one of, if not the most powerful, of the Protectors. I did not choose to lose him. He did. I will not change my mind." A sneer marred his handsome face. "Ah, it gets better."

"Release her arm at once, Julian." Both she and Julian turned toward the voice. Frosty eyes moved from Julian to Rachel. "We are not breaking this bond."

Great...Roderick was there.

Her Spartan practically flew across the room intent on tackling Julian to the ground. However, in the next instant, he stumbled back as if bouncing off an invisible shield.

"Why don't you wish to break the bond?" Julian seemed baffled, his head cocked to the side. With brows pinched, he waited for Roderick's reply.

Rachel started to argue, but Roderick's next words stopped her.

"Because I love her." He faced her. "I am in love with you Rachel and want to share my life with you."

For the first time Julian showed warmth of sorts, he uttered a soft chuckle. "The consequences of your actions will not be clear for a long time. I cannot grant you your wish to continue in the Protector force. You could be killed or worse cause one of the others to die. So, for now, the answer remains no." He met Rachel's gaze, the probing in his pointed stare, discomfiting. "The bond between you two must be completed now. The next in line will come."

"Is something wrong Rachel? What are you talking about Julian?" Roderick was instantly beside her, his eyes searching her face and then turning to Julian. "Tell me."

Without another word, Julian stalked out of the room.

She took a deep breath and framed his face with her hands. "Roderick, do you really love me?"

He nodded and leaned forward as if to kiss her, but her words stopped him.

"I am also in love with you. Rod, I'm pregnant."

His mouth opened and closed, and his eyebrows rose high but no words came out. Then his lips curved until a wide smile split his face. Yet at the same time, his eyes darted in the direction Julian had gone.

It was a bittersweet moment for him. He didn't have to tell her this.

"I never dreamed to start a family, not at this age. I cannot formulate the words to tell you what I am feeling right now. To find out you love me was more than I hoped, but to also find you are to give me the precious gift of my first child...I love you." He lifted her face up and kissed her. The presses of his lips, soft, gentle and precious. "Let's go."

"Are you sure?" Rachel said covering his large hands with hers. "Maybe we should remain and try to talk to him again. Surely he'll reconsider it. I can't believe he's letting you go."

"He'll come around. It may take him a couple years, but he will. Just need him to get over being pissed at me." There was warmth when he looked at her. "We have other things to do. Much to discuss. Let's get out of here." Although she didn't know Roderick as much as she'd hoped, it was interesting to her how patient he seemed to be with the Roman.

Rachel allowed Roderick to lead her from Julian's home. Although she did not see the Roman, she felt something as they went to her rental car. From one of the many windows he watched them. She was sure of it. Whether in anger or still puzzled, she didn't know, but one thing she did know. When she saw Julian again, once more, she'd beg him to reconsider.

CHAPTER EIGHT

RODERICK TRIED NOT to be angry at the entire situation. It was not fair. As hard as he tried to seem nonchalant for Rachel's sake, his gut churned at the thought of returning to Atlanta. Cyn would be paired up with someone else.

For lifetimes he's fought as a Protector, the war was far from over and every single fighter was required just to keep some semblance of control over the situation.

Needing time to adjust, he'd convinced Rachel to stay in Italy for a week. It would give Julian time to get his replacement and hopefully a few days for him to adjust to the idea of being benched.

His cell rang and he eyed the display. Rachel had gone out to the small villa's patio. From inside he could see her sitting in the sun with a glass of lemonade reading a book. She was the picture of serenity.

"Hey Cyn," he spoke in a quiet tone, "what's up?"

"What the fuck?" Cyn's voice exploded.

"You'll have to give me more of a clue." Roderick paced, the cursing in his ear making him cringe. His partner was livid.

Finally Cyn stopped the string of obscenities and formed a

sentence that made sense. "I've been partnered with James fucking Bond." The male's Scottish brogue became heavy with anger.

"Bond is cool."

"This fucker is not."

"Then call him something else."

Silence, he could see Cyn staring at the ceiling trying to come up with a better nickname. "I already kicked his ass once."

"What did he do?"

"Go back and see Julian. Tell him this shit is not going to work." Cyn said by way of an answer.

"Give the new guy a chance. I won't go back to Julian. Not for some time."

There was another long silence. Cyn read between the lines. Both of them knew Julian would not change his mind, not for a while. It could be a couple of years or it could be twenty. Nothing he could say at the moment would change their leaders' mind. "I'm weakening too fast. I can't put you or anyone in danger until this shit is controlled."

"Yeah." Cyn let out a breath. "Thor said once you get mated and live with her, you'd get straight."

Thor had never been mated. It would take a woman with a lot of patience or supersonic strength to tame that one. "How the hell would Thor know?"

"His last partner, another Viking, is mated."

Only Cyn would hold a conversation with Thor. "Besides, I called what's his name, the Spaniard. He said the same thing."

It touched him that his partner was scrambling to find a solution to his situation. "Thanks for that. I suspected as much. Since we've been together here, I notice a difference."

"Well anyway. I'll see you when you get back. We'll figure this out. Got your back."

Roderick nodded, even though Cyn couldn't see him, not trusting his voice.

"You okay?" Rachel stood at the door, her eyes pinned to his face. "Bad news?"

Manning up, he arranged his face into happy happy joy joy. "Nah, just Cynden being a pain as usual. He's mad about his new partner, some British guy."

"Do you know him?"

"Who?" He went to her and pulled her against him. Two reasons, she felt good there and it was hard to keep up the fake smile. She'd see through it.

"The British guy."

"Damn I forgot to ask his name. I know a couple British Protectors. Both are capable, very good."

"Want to go out to get a bite?" She looked up at him. At once he was lost in the pools of blue. Her beautiful lips moved, probably saying something important. But the only thing he heard was the thudding of his heart and the echo of blood rushing. She had become his everything, worth every loss. As long as she and his child were safe nothing would matter as much.

"Roderick?" She pouted and at once his attention came into focus. "You're ignoring me."

"Not at all. Yeah, so I didn't hear a word you said; I was too busy concentrating on your lips, your eyes, your face."

She softened, a sweet smile curving her lips. In that moment he vowed she'd always know how much he loved her. "Never doubt how I feel about you. Promise me."

Although she gave him a curious look, she nodded. "I promise."

"Because you are the single most important thing that's ever happened to me. The greatest gift."

She dug her face into his chest and wrapped her arms around his waist. "You're going to make me cry. That is so sweet." The words were muffled, but he felt an expansion in his chest when she let out a sigh and laid her head against him. "I love you so much."

There it was, the reason for his long life. It wasn't all the bullshit with Julian or even the demon slayer gig. His soul purpose was Rachel.

"I'll love you always, for eternity."

They left a few moments later, his entire being lighter at acknowledging how he truly felt.

"How do you know if someone is dark Fae?" Rachel asked as they strolled down a cobble-stoned street in Florence. He smiled as he'd spotted one not but a few moments earlier.

"They have a bluish tint to their skin. Humans can't see it."

She was thoughtful for a few beats. "Do you think I'll be able to see it?"

Good question, he thought. "I don't know. Probably not."

As they passed a small shop, Rachel tugged him toward it.

"Let's check out the pretty pottery."

RODERICK TOOK EVERYONE'S attention. Not just because he was a tall, broad-shouldered man, but because he was drop dead gorgeous.

It was hard to look away from him. Rachel figured it was how people that dated celebrities must feel like. Their partner getting all the attention, while they were more of a backdrop.

Only a couple days left in Italy and she'd yet to bring up the subject of their marriage or ask about the bonding ceremony. Each time she wanted to bring up the subject, a part of her was hurt that he'd not asked of his own free will. After all, he was the man and as old fashioned as it seemed, she wanted him to ask her and not have to bring it up.

Now standing inside the small ceramic shop in which he dwarfed the space and she immediately felt bad for him as he tried to maneuver about and not accidentally hit anything. "We can leave. I don't see anything I like," she lied eyeing a beautiful set of bowls.

"I think you should take your time and look about. I'll wait outside. I don't mind." He kissed her brow and left the shop having to bend down to get through the door.

"Grosso!" the shop owner exclaimed looking relieved as Roderick walked out. "Bello." She smiled.

"Si," Rachel grinned. Her man was very *bello* indeed.

A few minutes later she walked out into the bright afternoon sunshine. She'd purchased several items for her mother and Deborah, her friend, plus four bowls she planned to keep for herself. Roderick sat on a short wall that surrounded a beautiful fountain.

Something was off. Rachel wasn't sure how she knew. In spite of the cold air, there was a light sheen of perspiration on his upper lip and he wasn't looking her in the eye, but somewhere past her right shoulder. When he swallowed hard, she swiveled and checked behind. Nothing out of the norm.

"Rod? Are you all right?"

His smile was more of a grimace and he inhaled deeply. "Yeah why?"

"Because you look like you have a stomachache."

"Oh."

He took her packages and placed them on the short wall next to him. It could be Julian called him and offered him the job back. In exchange, Roderick would have to break up with her. If he was about to break up with her, then she'd take it with as much grace as possible. Once in the privacy of the villa, and away from him, she'd cry her eyes out.

"Is there something you have to tell me?"

He nodded and her stomach flipped. Then his face softened. Just as she was about to ask another question, her handsome man fell to his knees and held her hands up to his mouth kissing each knuckle.

His resplendent eyes met hers. "Rachel, I love you more than you'll ever know. I can't picture continuing life without you. That you carry my child is a blessing I never expected. Make me the happiest man alive and marry me."

It was her turn to swallow. The ground swayed and she let out a breath she'd been holding. "Of course I'll marry you. I love you so much." She threw her arms around his neck and pressed kisses to his face until their mouths met. He held her hard against him, his large strong body the warmest of refuges.

A moment later he dug in his pocket and brought out a ring. The stone sparkled in the sunshine and in spite of her happy tears; she noticed it was a huge pear shaped diamond set in a simple gold setting. He slipped it on her finger and she turned to the sound of applause and clicks of pictures being taken. The woman from the ceramic store clapped, smiling widely and cried out "Bravo!"

"Let's go back to the villa and celebrate in private," Roderick whispered in her ear and she turned his face to her and kissed him again. "Not until I get some gelato. You promised me gelato."

"You sure you want gelato now? It's freezing out here."

"Yep. I have to have it. Not sure if it's a craving or that it's so good. Even the cold won't stop me." She lifted a brow at him.

"As you wish beauty, but I think I'll find some hot steaming coffee."

She felt bad for him. "We don't have to walk to the gelato stand. I can wait."

His eyes were so full of love, she had to blink back tears again. "Oh you're getting it. Lots of it. I'm going to buy extra in case you want some later. Anything for you. All you have to do is ask and I will do it."

"Wow." Rachel sighed. "If this is a dream, I don't want to ever wake up."

They walked hand in hand back toward a gelato stand she'd spotted earlier. The holidays were upon them, the light breeze was crisp, and the bright decorations began lighting up as the shorter day came to an end.

Roderick glanced at her. "I love you."

She could only nod, her heart filled to overflowing.

CHAPTER NINE

"**W**HAT DO YOU think?" Rachel asked as she stepped back from the ten-foot Christmas tree. Her face tilted up as she studied the latest of many decorations she'd placed on its branches.

"It's perfect," Roderick told her and glanced at the other two men in the room, who also nodded.

His beautiful new wife frowned at them. "You guys keep saying that, or just nodding. Look at it, does one side have more ornaments than the other? How about the lights, are they well balanced? I don't want people to come over and it be all wonky."

"It's not wonky," Cyn said between bites of the pizza they'd ordered. "It's nice. A bit frilly, but nice."

"Frilly?" Rachel's voice rose an octave and all three of them froze.

"Now you've done it," Fallon Trent, the Brit and Cyn's new partner, muttered earning a glare from the Scot.

Roderick wanted to punch Cyn in the head, but figured it would only upset Rachel further. "We like frilly. It's good to have a female here to soften things."

"True," Cyn agreed with haste. "You make things smell

good too."

Rachel laughed and the men let out a collective breath.

For the first time in centuries, he looked forward to the holidays. He was married now and had been offered a position at the local hospital. Yes, it would be strange to work with humans and somehow keep them from noticing he was different. He would have to wear contacts to keep the luminescence of his eyes hidden and pretend not to notice any dark Fae when in the presence of humans. In spite of all the adjustments, he was happy.

Leaving Rachel to continue decorating, the men went into the home office. Roderick sat at his desk, Cyn and Fallon on a couch and a chair.

"They're organizing; forming some sort of coven. Some master level Fae is taking the helm," said Fallon Trent, an 1800s British lord, who remained every bit the dandy. Although now he dressed in modern clothing, Roderick ventured to guess every piece was expensive designer wear.

Cyn nodded. "Yeah dickhead and I followed some lesser ones and at dawn they traveled north toward Dahlonega. We lost them thanks to some trucker convoy." He motioned to Fallon who looked up at the ceiling.

It was bad news. They'd suspected for months something was up, but the dark Fae had kept it well hidden. Most of the trouble lately had been younger ones doing stupid stuff, not smart enough to hide. However with the rash of deaths in Atlanta lately were getting the police department's attention. Strange disappearances and reports of humans being chased by weird men, who moved so fast, they almost caught their car when driving away.

With an exhale, Roderick looked from one man to the other. "Does Julian know?"

The Brit nodded. "Yes, he is coming next week. Right now he's dealing with a problem in Ireland. Seems the light Fae are calling a summit of sorts. Julian is meeting with the Queen."

Cyn went to the bar and poured a drink. "Must be related to what's happening here." He motioned to the others and both shook their heads not wanting a drink. He met Roderick's gaze. "We need you, not enough of us to fight."

As if on queue his phone rang. It was Julian. Roderick put it on speaker. "Julian. The three of us are here in the same room." Roderick said by way of greeting.

The Roman's voice was measured. "I trust you are aware of what happens with the dark Fae. Several high level demons have joined resources and are forming groups, small parts of a larger army. The highest leader is somewhere in Europe." Julian paused. "I am sending another protector to join you. Not enough to fight all of them. Your role is to be guardians, not fighters. Only attack when a life is in danger."

"Who are you sending?" Cyn asked, his eyes on Roderick.

"Your brother Kieran."

"Five is not enough," Fallon said scowling. "We need Roderick back."

"Three," Julian interrupted. "Thor and Rowe are being transferred to New York. There is a larger army forming there." It sounded as if someone came into whatever room

Julian was in and he responded to whoever it was with a curt 'I'll be right there'.

Julian let out a breath. "Roderick you are not to be on the street unless I direct it."

Roderick bit back a curse. Instead he replied. "Very well."

The call ended without any further convo. They sat in the room in silence. They faced a new dynamic. Changes to the war against the dark Fae meant they'd have to be more alert.

"Guardians? What the fuck does that mean? I can't believe this shit." Cyn swallowed the amber liquid and got up to refill. "It's all kinds of fucked up."

It seemed both he and the Brit agreed as they asked for a drink this time.

CHAPTER TEN

T HE WEDDING WAS simple. More of a formality as far as Roderick was concerned. They'd already bonded by immortal law.

They stood in front of the Christmas tree with only the other Protectors, Rachel's friend Deborah and her parents as witnesses.

The friend and her father both slid wary glances towards the Protectors, obviously suspicious of Roderick's friends all being huge muscular men. They'd told them both the guys were all partners in a bodyguard business, but that didn't help instill a comfortable trust in them.

Rachel was beautiful in a long yellow off the shoulders gown. His bride didn't wear anything in her hair, leaving the golden brown waves to flow down her back. She held only a couple of white roses. A more beautiful bride he could not imagine.

Her nervous smile made him all giddy and he leaned over and kissed her.

"Hey wait until the whole husband and wife thing before you kiss her," Cyn said, helpful as always.

A pastor friend of Rachel's performed a quick ceremony

and a few minutes later, they were husband and wife.

"Merry Christmas," Roderick whispered in her ear when he slipped a delicate band on her finger. It was the most perfect gift ever.

RACHEL COULDN'T WAIT for everyone to leave. Cyn and his new partner had gone for the weekend to give them privacy, which was sweet. She walked into the bedroom and placed a vase with the roses on the dresser. Roderick's room looked totally different now. She'd added throw pillows to the bed, her perfume bottles and jewelry box adorned the top of the chest of drawers and there was a beautiful painting she'd brought from her home over the headboard.

Her Spartan entered the room, his beautiful eyes roaming her body. Instantly she wanted him touching her, over her. "You're still dressed."

"So are you," she countered with a smile. "Come here, let's do something about that."

Under his black suit jacket, he wore a button up pale blue shirt and black slacks. She'd never seen him dressed up like this. He was breathtaking. "I'm glad we'll have pictures of tonight. I'm going to frame them and put them everywhere."

His lips covered hers and he pulled back just enough to speak. "Can we talk about decorating later?" The sensation of the zipper lowering down her back was followed by the dress pooling at her feet.

Not taking her eyes from his, she unbuttoned his shirt with shaky fingers. While she pushed it off his shoulders, he unfastened his pants and pushed them off, and then in one fluid move, he scooped her off her feet and carried her to the bed.

He came over her, his long hair falling forward in a beautiful silver cascade. "I want you. Not sure I can be gentle right now." The gruffness in his voice sent every nerve in her body to tingle.

"I don't want gentle. Not this time." Rachel accentuated her statement by wrapping her long legs around his waist.

The meeting of their mouths was all heat and hunger, as if they'd not been together in forever. So much desire filled her, she began to shake needing him.

"Rod." It was all she could say. Thankfully the message was clear. The pronunciation of his name although so rough on her lips sounded erotic in her ears.

The nudging of his penis at her entry shot arrows of heat through her, pooling at her core. Rachel lifted her hips just as he thrust in.

"Yes! Please..." his mouth covered hers and his tongue dove in. Taking her completely as he pulled out of her and pushed back in.

She clutched first at his shoulders then needing more, slid her hands down his broad back and dug her fingernails into the taut skin of his butt.

Roderick was lost; the only reaction to her pleas and nails

biting into this skin was to move faster and deeper. His thickness filled her completely before pulling out leaving a trail of need. Overwhelming her every sense, his movements combined with the beauty of the man Rachel let go, unable to process it all. She screamed and flailed, unable to see anything other than the bursting of lights behind her eyelids.

On he continued, thrusting and pulling in and out continuing through her climax, the friction of it sending her once again to soar. Just as she thought she could barely stand it, he bit her.

"What?" She gasped at the sensation of him sucking at her neck. He held her head and shoulders steady while buried deep in her. When he pulled back, his eyes were darkened. "It was the last part of the bonding. I haven't told you, but we drop fangs when fighting or when mating."

A part of her wanted to shove him off, but then she saw it. The look. He was nervous, self-conscious.

From the corner of his lips a tiny drop of her blood trickled down and she watched it. "I want to see."

"What?" He knew what she asked. She was sure of it, but wanted her to say it.

"Your fangs"

"Are you sure?"

Rachel nodded. "Yes, I want to know everything about you Rod."

He opened his mouth and slowly his incisors grew, forming perfect, but quite long fangs.

"You bit me with those? It didn't feel like they were that

big."

"You were preoccupied."

"Hmm." She reached out with her finger and touched the tip. It pierced her skin, a bright red dot formed. Shocked at how sharp it was, her eyes widened. "Whoa, those are dangerous."

He smiled around the fangs and she grinned. "Wow just when I thought you couldn't get any hotter."

"Well, it's a good thing I'm not finished." He moved his hips and her mouth fell open in a loud gasp. She pulled her protector down for a kiss, careful of his fangs and pushed her hips up to take him deeper.

Minutes later, they were once again lost in the moment.

Six months later

"MOVE IT A bit over to the right," Rachel studied the placement of the crib, her pretty face pinched in concentration. "What do you think?"

Roderick came over to where she sat and pressed a kiss to her brow, his hand moving automatically to her swollen belly. "What I think doesn't matter. I want you to be happy."

The curve of her lips brightened the room, and he kissed her again lightly.

They'd set up a crib, small dresser and changing table in

the spare bedroom next to theirs. It was all set to be the baby's nursery.

He bent to pick up a framed photograph of them in Italy from its box. "I'm glad we got that couple to take a picture of us in Florence. I like to see this reminder of when we finally agreed to be together."

Her fingers traced across her swollen stomach and her eyes met his. "Yes, I had to have a souvenir of our honeymoon for the baby."

It was hard not to linger on the soft curve of her lips. She was getting uncomfortable, their child would be born soon, and so he'd kept from taking her in bed. The last time they'd made love although erotic, had been awesome until he'd stayed up the rest of the night worried he'd hurt her or the child. By her snores and deep sighs, Rachel slept soundly, seeming more content than contrite. Yet he vowed not to have sex until she delivered, which would be any day now.

"We did it kind of backwards don't you think? Honeymoon before the wedding." Roderick laughed and broke his train of though. "But it worked for us."

Rachel slid to the edge of the seat and he helped her to her feet.

She took the picture from him and held it up against the wall over the crib; she turned to look at him. "What do you think?"

Love for her and the happiness she'd brought into his long and lonely life filled him. He could only nod in response, words not getting past the knot in his throat.

Her eyes softened. "I'm glad you are able to take a couple days off from the hospital to help me set up the nursery. Our son will be here soon and I want everything just right."

She watched him hammer a nail into the wall and carefully hang the picture. He turned to see her eyes had filled with tears.

He came closer to cradle her in his arms, and pushed the hair out of her face. "What's wrong sweetheart?"

"You hate your new job don't you?" She sniffed and pushed her face into the space between his neck and shoulder. "Because of me and all that mess with the stupid demon, you can't do what you were destined to. I know you miss being a Protector. Hate being stuck at the hospital while Cyn and Fallon do whatever it is they do."

"I don't hate being a doctor. I save lives instead of taking them, it's rewarding. And I still help the guys out when they need me. Besides, not putting my life in danger on a regular basis means I'll definitely be around for you and the baby."

"That's true." With a wide smile she threw her arms around his neck and pulled his face to hers. "I love you so much," she pressed kisses all over his face.

A chuckle escaped and she frowned up at him.

"What's so funny?"

"That I never thought I could be so happy. I'll love you forever." He said, not quite being honest. He wasn't sure of her reaction to him thinking it comical how pregnancy affected her emotions.

"Oh Rod, you make me so happy." Rachel sighed against

him.

That after all these years he'd found a renewed purpose in life beside a woman, didn't cease to surprise him.

Yes, he missed spending his nights out on the Atlanta streets battling those that sought to hurt innocents, but he wouldn't trade his life with Rachel and the son he'd soon meet for anything in the world.

Perhaps Julian would change his mind one day and allow him to join the Protectors again. For now, he accepted the punishment. Such as it was.

Secretly he hoped the Roman would not seek his sword arm until his son was old enough to understand. Especially since one day his son could possibly join the Protectors himself.

There would be no choice; a son sired by a Protector was usually predestined. Rachel didn't know yet. There was plenty of time for that conversation.

"I'm hungry." His beautiful wife tugged his hand toward the kitchen. "Want some ice cream?"

Roderick followed her from the room. "Anything is good as long as I share it with you."

Her delighted giggle died as his lips moved over hers. Then she grabbed his shoulders and pulled him tight against her.

"I can't wait until we can have wild monkey sex again." She murmured against his lips. "I miss seeing you naked."

"Want me to strip?" He offered.

Rachel laughed. "A strip tease and ice cream. Now that is every woman's dream come true."

EPILOGUE

– Read only if you won't be bothered by a cliffhanger... okay you've been warned!

Sixteen years later

"**B**ROCK!" RACHEL CALLED from the kitchen. "Sweetheart, please answer the house phone, it might be your dad." She finished slicing cucumbers and tossed them into the salad bowl. Once the salad was finished, she'd pour a glass of wine and relax until dinnertime.

She glanced through the opening of the kitchen towards the family room where Brock played a video game. The house phone rang again. "Get the phone!" she yelled louder in case he wore headphones.

Ever since he'd been grounded from using his cell phone, the house phone rang nonstop. Some kind of punishment it turned out to be. The phone calls never stopped.

Any calls she got came to her cell directly.

The insistent ringing stopped and she let out a sigh.

Her chest constricted and she frowned. For some reason she'd been on edge all day barely able to concentrate. She wrapped the salad bowl with plastic wrap and placed it in the refrigerator.

She'd call Roderick and ensure all was well Rachel thought looking around the space for her cell.

"Brock, do you see my phone?" She called out. Instead of a reply, the lanky boy walked in holding the cell phone out to her. She eyed his mused hair, the same striking silver as his father's. Brock blew a lock out of his eyes. "It's Uncle Cyn; he says it's important."

"Son, comb your hair. It's almost time for your dad to get home. We'll have dinner then." Rachel waited for him to leave before bringing the phone to her ear.

"How are you Cyn?" She heard Roderick's closest friend clear his throat and her stomach clenched. "What's wrong?"

"Roderick's been taken."

The stilted words filtered past the shock and ringing in her ears only to confuse her. Surely she'd misheard him. "What did you say? That's not possible, he called earlier and said he was going into surgery."

"He must have gone outside the hospital this afternoon. Maybe someone called him to come out, or could have taken a break. Hell I don't know."

She stumbled backwards and stuck out a hand grabbing the counter to steady herself. "How can you be sure he was taken? Did someone see something?"

"Yeah, there was a call to the local authorities by a hysterical nurse who witnessed several men grabbing Roderick and forcing him into the back of a van." His voice cracked. "Rachel I'm sorry, but from the details, we're sure it was demons."

"Why would they take him? He's not working with you

right now. It makes no sense."

"Which made it easier for them to do so. His guard was down. I can't see any other way they could have done it. Roderick is one of the strongest Protectors. They had to have done something or said something that made it easy to get him to go with them. I was worried about Brock until he answered the phone."

She let out a breath. "What happens now?"

"Julian is on his way here to Atlanta. Just make sure you keep Brock inside. I'm going to patrol with Fallon. Kieran will head there shortly," he said referring to his brother. "Turn on the alarm system."

All breath left her body and she collapsed onto a chair, her eyes jerking to the doorway hoping Brock did not overhear. "Cyn be honest with me, is he alive?" She whispered.

"I don't know."

Find out the what happens next in *Immortal Highlander*, the first full length story in the Protectors Series.

Immortal Highlander....

IMMORTAL HIGHLANDER
CHAPTER ONE

E MMA BLAKE FELT at home in the shadows. It was where she survived, always concealing the truth from those around her.

Now as she hid in the doorway of an abandoned building, she couldn't help but compare the current situation to her life.

The dampness of the brick wall behind her seeped through to her skin, as she pushed further into the shade it provided to avoid being noticed. The putrid smell of trash and urine barely registered as the scene unfolding mesmerized her.

What happened in that moment evoked images of the endless battles dark and light forces had been waging since the dawn of time.

Although beautiful to behold, the warrior who fought before her wasn't exactly an angel, but he was as close to one as she would ever get. Emma took a big chance sticking around because once he noticed her presence; there would be one of two possibilities for her.

He would either help her or kill her.

The air blew chilly on this damp, drizzly day in Atlanta. A city that for some unknown reason, in the last few years, had become a hotbed for the dark Fae, or as most prefer to call them, demons. With such an influx of demons, human assaults were on the rise.

Emma continued to watch from the shelter of the doorway as the Protector fought his aggressors, ten huge, low-level demons armed with medieval-type swords.

She tensed, but didn't flinch as a demon's severed arm flew past her and hit the ground next to her foot with a sickening thud.

In her mind, there was no doubt as to whom the victor would be in the end. The fluidity of the Protector's movements and the speed of the fight enthralled her. Her gaze locked on his thick biceps. Muscles bulged on his right arm as he swung his sword in a seemingly effortless motion. Impressive, for the weapon he wielded had to weigh at least twenty pounds.

He dodged a blow and struck out with his sword to slash through one demon's chest. A dagger flew from his left hand and found its target in another's heart.

He already fought the next opponent as both demons fell.

The Protector was magnificent—she had to give him that. He was one of an army of immortal warriors trained for battle against demons. They kept a low profile from humans to avoid discovery. Yet anyone who happened upon them in battle would most likely mistake them for angels.

Avenging angels.

As she watched the Protector now, Emma could under-stand why people would make that assumption. He was not an angel, but a warrior that fought for good. His golden skin glistened from the rain as he fought. His long blonde hair flew around him like a halo as he swung his sword.

His face was a masterpiece that God surely had enjoyed creating. Perfectly arched eyebrows framed his ice-blue eyes. A shallow cleft softened his strong jaw. The sensuality of his full lips was not diminished by the snarl that remained constant as he battled.

Two demons left.

One of them looked in her direction. Did he see her?

No. I'm well hidden in this doorway.

Emma didn't panic. The demon was more worried about his survival at this point than feeding on her blood. The best option for him would be to run and save himself, while the Protector was distracted fighting another.

He chose self-preservation. Scant seconds later, the scent of the demon's fear assaulted her nostrils as he raced past her.

The demon disappeared around the corner, and she debated the advantages of running as well. Once enraged, only a fool would stick around and try to talk to a Protector. They were slow to calm.

She was one of the few that could see both Protectors and demons in their true forms.

Because of her demon heritage, she was also the Protector's mortal enemy.

The soft plop of droplets from the overhang splashing into puddles alerted her to the sudden silence. Emma froze and held her breath. The thumps of her heart echoed in her ears, yet she chanced a peek.

The Protector stood very still. He no longer fought. The body of the last demon lay at his feet, its blue blood pooled around his boots. In the next instant the body evaporated into a translucent blue vapor and swirled around the magnificent male.

Emma swallowed hard as the Protector raised his head to sniff the air. His actions slow and steady, as if he knew someone stood nearby. His frosty stare began to scan the alley, his eyes narrowed in her direction. She let out a breath of relief when he peered down at his left shoulder. He grimaced as he rotated it. One of the demons had gotten lucky. A bloodstain seeped through his gray t-shirt. He lifted the sleeve up and studied the wound, as if oblivious to her presence. He applied pressure with his right hand for a few moments. When he moved his hand away, the bleeding had stopped.

Emma shrank back when he raised his head and glanced in her direction again.

All air left her lungs when he stalked toward her with an alert expression, as if he expected her to flee in terror before he reached her. The thought did cross her mind.

As the Protector came closer, Emma gritted her teeth and balled up her fists to keep from running in the opposite direction. Her heart thumped inside her chest.

His face remained expressionless. He kept his hands re-laxed at his sides. His movements smooth but methodical. His sword, no longer drawn, was sheathed in a scabbard and slung across his broad back.

Fear surged again when the Protector stopped a few feet from her. Her blood ran cold and she could not suppress a tremble when his ice-blue eyes locked with her own and his nostrils flared. Narrowed eyes skimmed over her.

If he sensed demon first, she was dead.

At this distance, the male was magnificent. Now so close, he towered over her, at least six four and the male exuded pure power.

Emma remained tense and mentally cursed as fear seized her while she waited for his reaction. This was it, time to confront the man she'd been seeking for so long.

Protectors had more strength than demons and although her demon half made her stronger than most humans, no way in hell could she hope to defend herself if he decided to attack.

CYN PUSHED FURY aside, and took a deep breath to calm. He wasn't in the mood for more surprises. The low-levels that attacked him were less than a threat. What infuriated him the most was that he allowed the ambush.

Now a female waited for him, a small one at that. Just what he needed, another annoyance to deal with.

He'd taken his time pretending to inspect the cut to his shoulder, giving her time to run away.

She hadn't.

Interesting.

At this point, he didn't care if she'd seen him fight demons. Who would believe her anyway? As he stalked towards her, her eyes widened and she shuddered, but then squared her shoulders and held her ground.

Even more interesting, the petite woman barely flinched when Cyn stopped just a couple feet away and studied her.

Who was she?

The longer he watched her, the more frightened she appeared. Her heartbeat picked up, her lips parted, and her breathing accelerated. He inhaled the familiar scent of fear. Could she have witnessed what had just transpired between him and the low-level demons?

Regardless, she was afraid of him.

His inner voice urged him to erase her memory and move on. Curiosity stopped him.

He tried to determine what she was. She didn't seem like a demon. Her skin lacked the telltale blue tinge visible to Protectors.

Fully human? Perhaps, but he doubted it.

Cyn leaned forward and peered into her honey-brown eyes as he tried to read her thoughts.

He could not.

She could be one of the few humans that were difficult to read, or did she intentionally block him?

This is trouble. Move on.

Once again, he ignored the voice in his head.

The woman swallowed, but didn't budge; as if afraid he'd attack at her slightest move. Not a bad assumption on her part.

He took advantage of her stillness, Cyn's eyes traveled over her body again. In her gray business suit and conservative black pumps, she looked like she'd just stepped away from an office. Certainly, there were better places for her to be than this alley on such a damp, dreary day. Almost as if in response to his thoughts, a rumble of thunder boomed over them.

Both ignored it.

The woman became increasingly nervous as he continued to study her. Her breaths now came in small pants as she shuffled, putting weight on one leg and then the other. Her hand shook slightly when she raised it to brush several strands of golden brown hair away from her flushed, heart shaped face.

Pretty was not an adequate word to describe her. She was exquisite. His eyes lingered on her lips.

How would her lips feel under mine?

The fact that she took his breath away gave Cyn pause. After hundreds of years and many attractive women in his bed, it was rare that beauty affected him so intensely.

The female narrowed her eyes at him and her nostrils flared. She interrupted his thoughts. "I know this is probably not the best time, but I need to talk to you. There's no one else who can do what you do. I need your help."

Cyn's interest spiked as she spoke. No accent, so that didn't help him.

He didn't answer her. Instead, he inhaled deeply and concentrated on isolating her scent that floated in the air. She smelled of tropical islands, a hint of coconut mixed with her natural essence. The heady fragrance forced him to take a step back. His entire body reacted to her.

Definitely time to leave.

Like any normal male, it wasn't unusual for him to become aroused in the presence of an attractive female. But this reaction was different. It was intoxicating. Unlike any other he could remember.

His heartbeat quickened, his hands tingled urging him to reach out and touch her. A rush of heat coursed through his body. A feeling not too different from what he experienced in battle, but this time lust, not rage caused it. He couldn't tear his eyes away from her.

The female appeared normal. Yet something about her that he couldn't quite explain pulled at him.

A witch? He didn't believe so.

Another type of immortal? He hoped not. He'd have to kill her if she posed a threat to humans.

She seemed to sense his thoughts, and took a step back. "Can we go somewhere to talk?" she asked him in a confident voice.

When he reached out to touch her, she held her hands up defensively. "Wait, don't kill me. Just give me a couple minutes to explain…."

"Believe me, sweetheart, killing you is not exactly what I have in mind right now." His fingers curled around her forearm and he drew her to him.

She yelped as if his touch burned her. She tried to yank her arm from his hold and glared at him. Her eyes flickered to his hand. "Let go of me, you're hurting me. Just please let me talk to you, it's very important that I tell you something."

The woman was either crazy or very brave to stand up to

him. He released her forearm but kept his hand on her shoulder, to make sure she didn't bolt. "Alright, talk."

Before speaking, she eyed the hand on her shoulder. "My…. my sister, she's been taken and I need your help to save her. Demons took her hostage. I know you can help her. You're sworn to protect innocents." Her bottom lip quivered, it made him wonder if she acted the part, but the plea in her eyes gave him a jolt.

He hated how she fogged his ability to think straight. He shook his head to clear it.

"I don't do rescues," he snapped. "Why are you really here? Who are you?"

"I just told you, I'm a woman who's desperate enough to come to you for help," she replied.

He studied her for a moment longer before her eyes slid away from his and focused on his lips.

All of a sudden he was able to hear her thoughts. *"His mouth, it's so perfect…"*

His gaze fell to hers.

Thunder clapped simultaneously as he gave in to the powerful connection and drew her to him, ignoring her surprised gasp.

His mouth crushed hers. Caught off guard, she parted her lips and he dove in allowing his tongue to explore. She responded almost immediately. The woman clutched his arms and leaned into him. He hardened, aroused at the lush pliant body pressed against him.

With strength that belied her size, she ran her hands up

from his forearms to his shoulders and drew him closer. Her lips were as soft as the rest of her. The woman's entire body molded into his now, and the warmth of it enveloped him. He closed his eyes and allowed the wonderful feel of her to consume him. He deepened the kiss as his hands traveled down her back and cupped her butt. When he ground his hardness into her, he was rewarded by a soft moan.

Time seemed to stop as his lips traveled over her mouth. Aroused beyond thought, his fangs dropped and he used the tips to tease her bottom lip.

The tingling on the back of his neck, alerted him of a demon presence nearby. The defensive warning jolted him back to reality. He broke the kiss and raised his head to look around while he held her against him. The sound of their heavy breathing filled the quiet of the alley until a growl came from deep in his throat.

More demons and they were headed for them.

"Damn it," he said, reluctant to move away from her.

When he released her, the woman swayed, blinking repeatedly. An expression of shock and disgust crossed her face. Her upper lip curled and she covered her mouth with her hands. "Oh God! I can't believe I let you kiss me."

Cyn ignored her comment at first. "Demons are headed this way. You gotta go," he told her and then narrowed his eyes at her and added, "and for the record, you not only let me kiss you, but you kissed me back."

Putting her hands on his chest she shoved him away. A light blush confirming she'd indeed enjoyed the kiss.

She narrowed those beautiful honey brown eyes at him. "What did you expect? You killed a bunch of demons. They are going to send an army after you now."

He shrugged. "So, what else is new?"

This female was spunky.

Too bad he'd never see her again.

He bowed his head at her. "Nice meeting you."

Turning away, he rushed towards his Harley.

"WAIT!" EMMA HELD up both hands and shouted as the Protector ran toward a massive black and chrome motorcycle. He hesitated for a second and she thought he'd heard her.

But, without a backward glance, he straddled the seat and sped off.

"Damn it! Now I have to find him all over again." She jerked around and scanned the alleyway. He'd said demons were headed there. It wouldn't be good to be there alone when they arrived. She hurried out of the alley.

She felt foolish. After all that work to find the Protector and getting up the nerve to talk to him, she didn't even get the chance to tell him the rest of the information. It'd taken her almost a week to find him. Night after night spent skulking through shadowy alleys and streets, following demons all over Atlanta.

Now she was forced to start all over again. She dropped her head, and allowed exhaustion to take over.

It began to rain harder so she hurried across the street toward her office.

Minutes later, Emma sat at her functional wooden desk at Georgia Bank and Trust with her chin in her hands and stared at the bleary words on the papers in front of her. Her thoughts were far away.

When she found him again, she would not allow her attraction to the Protector to hinder her. Her priority was to find her sister.

Emma opened her eyes and scanned the almost empty bank lobby through the glass office walls. The wet weather kept most customers home this day.

It was her last day at the bank. She'd requested an extended leave of absence. With no appointments scheduled, the rest of her afternoon loomed ahead.

Since Briana's kidnapping, the days had been unbearable for her. It was hard to concentrate at work while the demons held Briana. She didn't want to imagine what her sister was going through at the hands of the evil beings.

Hostage, until she brought the *ransom*.

Now, after she'd failed to convince Cynden Fraser to help her, a heavy sense of hopelessness engulfed her.

"What happened?" Wendy, her friend and coworker asked from the doorway. She didn't wait for an answer and walked in closing the door behind her. Wendy plopped down on a chair with a hopeful expression on her face. Wendy leaned forward, her vivid green eyes searching Emma's face, as she waited for her answer. Emma's mood lightened.

Wendy was one of a handful of humans Emma had ever met who knew about demons and Protectors. Wendy was attacked by a demon one night and a Protector rescued her. Although she'd never seen the Protector again, Wendy could describe him in great detail, which she did every chance she got. By Wendy's description, the Protector who rescued her had an uncanny resemblance to Cynden, except for the eye color. She swore her rescuer had clear green eyes. Cynden's eyes were a very definite shade of blue.

It was very strange that Wendy could remember in great detail what happened to her almost two years earlier. As a rule, Protectors were careful after a rescue to erase the human's memories of a demon attack. Although Emma didn't understand why Wendy's memory remained intact, she was grateful to have a friend to confide in.

As their friendship grew, Emma shared more and more about the Protectors. When she confessed her own demon bloodline, Wendy accepted her disclosure without judgment and their friendship became stronger.

Head still resting in her hands, Emma answered Wendy's question. "I found Cynden, the Protector. But he refused to help me."

"Really? You gotta be kidding me. I thought they're supposed to rescue humans, or... innocent beings, from demons." Wendy frowned and bit her bottom lip in thought before she continued. "What did you say? What did he say?"

"I told him that my sister is being held hostage by demons and that I needed his help. He said," she deepened her voice, "'I don't do rescues,' and left before I could say anymore. Now I have to find him all over again."

Eyes stinging with tears, Emma threw her hands up in exasperation. "Every day that passes can only be more torturous for poor Briana."

"You'll find him again Emma. I'll help you," Wendy said. Then she stilled and studied Emma, her brow crinkled. "Good thing you don't have any customers, you're a mess."

Emma's hands flew to her hair, she hadn't even thought about straightening herself up after the encounter with the Protector. "It's windy and drizzling out there," she replied, hoping her discomfort wasn't obvious.

She could feel her friend's stare as she took out a compact mirror to check her hair and make-up. Her lipstick smudged from one side of her mouth to her cheek and her hair was disheveled.

"I'm sorry. I'm sure your makeup is the last thing on your mind right now," Wendy said.

Emma's cheeks warmed as she thought about Cynden's kiss. She grabbed for a tissue and wiped at her stained mouth harder than necessary. Wendy didn't seem to notice her discomfort and continued to talk, "Don't worry, we'll find him again and explain everything. Then I'm sure he'll agree to help to you. I'll even help you search for him. Remind him that he is supposed to help. He took an oath."

Emma couldn't help but smile at Wendy's stern expression. "I'll do that."

Wendy's face softened as she gave Emma a reassuring smile. "Briana is in all probability doing okay. You told me yourself, she'd been hanging out with demons lately. She might even know some of the demons that took her."

"These demons are not the BFF type, and it's Gerard, a Master demon that has Briana," Emma replied, but she hoped more than anything Wendy was right.

The lobby doors opened and a pair of customers shuffled in and shook the rain off their coats and umbrellas. Both headed to the tellers.

Although she and Briana were like night and day, Emma adored her sister.

Just months earlier, Emma suspected that Briana was going to Inferno, a local nightclub, and known demon hangout. She'd tried on several occasions to talk to her sister about the danger of being around too many demons, but Briana laughed off her concerns and called her a bore.

The fact that being in the company of full-blooded demons presented the possibility of her demon side taking over was a thrill Briana couldn't resist.

Now Briana was in trouble. Big trouble.

Hostage, until Emma lured Cyn to the demons. He was the price she was to pay.

The ransom.

END OF EXCERPT

ABOUT THE AUTHOR

Writing is my dream come true. There is nothing I love more than bringing my characters and stories to life and sharing them with you. Writing paranormal romance is a rewarding and enjoyable part of my life.

I live in a large town in Georgia with my super hero husband and three unruly little dogs.

If you enjoyed Immortal Spartan, please recommend it to your friends and family. And if you have time, I would sincerely appreciate a review.

I love hearing from my readers and am always excited when you join my newsletter to keep abreast of new releases and other things happening in my world. Newsletter sign up:

Other H.M. McQueen (Hildie McQueen) Links:

Website: www.HMMcQueen.com

Facebook: facebook.com/PNRMcQueen